"You can't h̲a̲[ve]
without a br[...]

"That is a slight problem," Jax admitted. "But only a slight one."

"It doesn't sound so slight to me," Kara insisted. "If you and Anabel are still at odds..." Her head was spinning.

"Well, except for one small thing, every piece is already in place."

"*One small thing?* The *bride?* What are you going to do? Advertise? Hold a lottery?"

He shrugged. "You're the expert planner."

Kara swallowed hard. "You want me to find you a wife?"

"There is somebody who'd be suitable."

"Who?" Kara mused. "An old girlfriend of yours?"

"Not exactly. I meant you."

Almost at the altar—
will these *nearlyweds* become *newlyweds*?

Welcome to Nearlyweds, our brand-new miniseries
featuring the ultimate romantic occasion—weddings!
Yet these are no ordinary weddings: our beautiful brides
and gorgeous grooms only *nearly* make it to the altar—
before fate intervenes and the wedding's...*off!*

But the story doesn't end there....
Find out what happens in these tantalizingly emotional
novels by some of your best-loved Harlequin Romance®
authors over the coming months.

Look out in March for
His Runaway Bride
by Liz Fielding

THE BRIDAL SWAP
Leigh Michaels

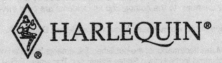

TORONTO • NEW YORK • LONDON
AMSTERDAM • PARIS • SYDNEY • HAMBURG
STOCKHOLM • ATHENS • TOKYO • MILAN • MADRID
PRAGUE • WARSAW • BUDAPEST • AUCKLAND

ISBN 0-373-03637-X

THE BRIDAL SWAP

First North American Publication 2001.

Copyright © 1999 by Leigh Michaels.

Visit us at www.eHarlequin.com

Printed in U.S.A.

CHAPTER ONE

THE throaty hum of the sewing machine and the whispery hush of yard after yard of satin sliding under the needle blended with the creak of the rocking chair into a hypnotic rhythm that filled the duplex's living room. Kara Schuyler glanced at the mantel clock and then down at the six-week-old baby sleeping in her arms and wished she didn't have to leave.

Rhonda didn't look up from the pool of orchid satin, which under her skillful fingers was slowly becoming a formal gown. "Let me get this straight. The wedding of the century is only two weeks off, and you *still* haven't met the groom?"

Her friend's tone was skeptical, and Kara sighed. "There's nothing really unusual about that," she pointed out. "Most of the time it's the bride who makes the wedding plans, and she's the one who hires me. And in this case..."

Rhonda finished a seam and shifted the fitted bodice into position to start the next one. "I suppose the gazillionaire's too busy to be bothered."

"It wouldn't be surprising, would it? As soon as Jax Montgomery figured out how to sell sunshine, he started trying to make every consumer product in the world solar powered."

"Since he's so preoccupied, I'm amazed he's finding time to get married at all." Suddenly, Rhonda let her hands drop from the dress as she stared at Kara in mock horror. "You don't suppose he'll delegate his personal assistant to stand in for him on the honeymoon—do you?''

Kara slid to the edge of her seat and shifted the baby's weight. ''The honeymoon, no. The ceremony, on the other hand… Well, I'd give it a pass myself if I could.''

''You? Wedding planner extraordinaire? If you're tired of holding Dylan, just put him in the bassinet.''

''I don't think I could ever get tired of holding him, but I have to meet the incredible Anabel for lunch and an update on the wedding plans.'' Kara laid the child down. He grunted a little and pursed his lips as if in search of a bottle, and she bent over to rub his tummy till he relaxed. ''Normally, the bigger the event the more interesting it is. But last week when she recruited her thirteenth bridesmaid…''

Rhonda rolled her eyes. ''*And* added yet another shade of purple to the palette… Did I tell you what kind of rush charges my supplier demanded in order to promise I'll have that bolt of fabric in time?''

''You mentioned it. Be sure to give me the bill so I can add it to Anabel's stack.''

''Don't worry.'' Rhonda's tone was dry. ''Since I had to pay in advance, I'm not going to forget it any time soon. In fact, the bill's at the top of the pile, right there on the coffee table.''

Kara reached for a yellow receipt and raised her eyebrows at the total. ''This one? I see what you mean. If I take it right now, I'll probably have your money this afternoon.''

''The sooner it's paid, the better Jeff will like it. With his tuition due this month, there wasn't any extra money, so I cashed in the baby's gift certificates to pay the rush charges—and he wasn't very pleased with me.''

''I will say this much for the incredible Anabel,'' Kara

mused. "She never flinches at the bills. I'll tell her that the bridesmaids' dresses are all coming along just fine—right?"

"As fine as they can when all thirteen of the young ladies in question seem to be on diets. At the present rate, I'm likely to be taking tucks while the procession's waiting at the back of the church."

"No church. Didn't I tell you? The wedding's going to be in the main ballroom at the Century Club."

"And here I was expecting a cathedral at the very least." Rhonda sat back from the sewing machine. "As long as we're talking about clothes, what's with you today, Kara? I've never thought of you as the little-navy-blue-dress type."

Kara brushed a hand down over her slim skirt. "What's so bad about my dress? Not too long, not too short. Classic...appropriate...subdued..."

"Not to say dull and matronly."

The corner of Kara's mouth quirked. "It seemed to reflect the sort of image Anabel expects from me."

"Is she that much of a snob? I know the Schuyler name carries a certain cachet around this town, but surely she knows better than to think you're so prim and proper you can't be stylish. Doesn't she?"

"Well, she hired me to give her a classy wedding, not to try to compete with her personal *savoir faire.*"

"Not that you could, of course."

"Thanks for your delightful candor," Kara murmured. "But must you rub salt in the wound?"

Rhonda shrugged. "It's true. You're not bad-looking at all, Kara, but next to her... The woman didn't get to the finals of the Miss World pageant by accident."

"And I suppose she'd go into peals of laughter at the mere idea that I might be trying to outshine her. Or more likely, to make someone else think I was trying to out-shine her.''

''And what if you actually succeeded?'' Rhonda's eyes lit with delight. ''*That's* why she hasn't let you meet the gazillionaire,'' she gasped. ''Because she's afraid you might take him away from her!''

Kara left her car in a distant corner of the Century Club's parking lot and walked across to the main entrance. The day was gorgeous, even for mid-May; the breeze was soft and warm against her face, and the scent of lilacs drifted from the thick hedge that separated the first tee of the golf course from the wide lawn of the elegant old mansion that served as a clubhouse.

The elderly doorman, his uniform spotless and his bearing as straight as ever, greeted her with a smile. ''We still have valet service, Miss Kara, and the boys would be happy to park your car.''

''It's too beautiful to be inside any more than necessary. And since I'm early—'' She caught a warning in his eyes. ''What's wrong, Curtis?''

''Miss Randall arrived a few minutes ago.''

Startled, Kara eyed her wristwatch. Either it was running slow and therefore she had an apology to make, or the unthinkable had happened and Anabel Randall was actually early for an appointment.

For once Kara ignored the delicate curve of the branching staircase that soared upward from the elegant foyer to the most private retreats the clubhouse offered, focusing her gaze instead on the enormous grandfather clock that stood off to one side. Relieved to see she was exactly on time, she turned toward the double doors leading to the main dining room. The maître d' wasn't at his post, but he'd no doubt be back any moment, and he'd know whether Anabel was already seated in the dining room or was waiting for her in the lounge overlooking the formal gardens and swimming pool at the back of the clubhouse.

A door slammed upstairs, and the sudden crash drew Kara's attention—and her eyebrows—upward. A member having a tantrum? Surely not; that sort of thing was frowned on at the Century Club. It must have been just a stray breeze.

But the bang of the door had scarcely faded before firm, hasty footsteps sounded on the upper landing and a statuesque brunette appeared at the top of the stairs. Kara bit back a smile. After a few months of working with Anabel Randall, she knew the routine well. The beauty queen always paused at the top of a flight of steps just long enough to draw all eyes, then she floated down with her head high and her back straight, seeming to barely touch each step as she descended.

This time, however, to Kara's surprise, Anabel obviously wasn't interested in making an entrance. She didn't even look around to check out her audience, just hurried down the long flight and brushed past Kara on her way to the front door. Her chin was high, her face was hard, and her eyes glittered. She was still gorgeous—but she looked ten years older than the last time Kara had seen her.

Kara called her name twice before Anabel paused. She hesitated for a fraction of a second, then slowly turned. "Oh, it's you. I forgot you were going to be here."

That didn't bode well, Kara thought. For Anabel to be early for an appointment and then forget it entirely—and not just a casual get-together, but a standing weekly date concerning her wedding, the most important event in her life this year...

"What is it?" Kara asked. "Is someone ill? Injured? Can I help?"

Anabel laughed harshly. "Jax should be grateful he isn't injured." She tossed a smoldering look up the stairs. "After what he just did... As for your helping, I suppose we might as well get this cleared up right now. But not right here. The last thing I want is to see that...jerk... again."

Kara's mouth went dry. *That jerk?* Anabel meant Jax Montgomery, of course. The gazillionaire fiancé. The man who was —or at least had been—the love of Anabel's life.

Obviously, he was upstairs right now. And just as obviously whatever had happened between them up there had been a disaster of herculean proportions.

Kara tried to fit the pieces together. Anabel had arrived early for her lunch date, something no one who knew her would have anticipated. And she had found her fiancé...doing what?

This can't be happening, Kara thought. Without a word, she followed Anabel out onto the veranda.

Without a word, Anabel thrust a set of car keys at Curtis. Then she turned her back on the doorman and took a deep breath. "The wedding's off."

Even though she'd known that announcement had to be coming, Kara hadn't braced herself well enough; the words hit like sledgehammers. "But why?"

Anabel's gaze was icy. "Surely you don't believe that *why* is any of your business?"

Kara cursed her delinquent tongue. She knew better than to ask; of course she did. She was only Anabel's employee, after all—not her friend.

However, Anabel's refusal to answer was in itself an interesting response. While she wasn't the sort to get

chatty with the hired help, Anabel had confided a few
intimate details along the way—enough that Kara knew
it wasn't purely principle that was keeping her silent.

So what had Jax Montgomery done that was not only
bad enough for Anabel to call off the engagement but so
wounding that she wouldn't even hint at the cause?

"It's off," Anabel snapped. "That's all you need to
know." She strode down the front steps. "How long does
it take to get a car around here anyway?" she barked at
Curtis.

Kara followed her. "But you can't just cancel a wedding." She winced at the sound of her own naive words.
"I mean, of course you can, but it's not like calling off
a tennis date. There's a tremendous amount of work involved in bringing everything to a halt—"

"That's your job. You get to be a wedding *unplanner*
for a change."

"And are you even certain you want to? Just because
the two of you have had a spat…"

Anabel turned on her, and the blaze in her eyes threatened to char Kara's skin.

Kara dismissed the possibility that Anabel was keeping
silent out of remaining loyalty to her fiancé, and she
raised her estimate of Jax Montgomery's misbehavior by
a factor of three. Had Anabel caught him with a harem,
for heaven's sake? Deliberately, she softened her voice.
"I just meant this is a pretty big decision, Anabel. It can't
hurt to give it a little time, to be sure it's what you want
to do—"

"The wedding is off." Anabel's words were crisply
spaced. "Cancel it. And I don't want to hear another word
about the entire subject, ever." Her convertible drew up
in front of the steps and the valet leaped out as if he'd
been sitting in a bonfire. Anabel slid behind the wheel.

Kara put her hand on the door before Anabel could close it. "Just a minute. It's not that simple. I can't just make one phone call and—"

"Why should I care how many phone calls it takes? That's your job, so do it."

"And there will be expenses involved in the cancellation. You've paid deposits, of course, but you can't just leave the people you've hired high and dry. The contracts you signed specify fees in case of a change of plans. I don't have the totals with me, but—"

Anabel laughed. "Oh, really? I'm supposed to pay them for doing nothing? They can get other jobs if they're as wonderful as you told me they were. Not that it matters—if you think I'm throwing another dime down the drain over this affair, you're wrong. Now get out of my way."

The engine roared, and Kara leaped back just as the BMW shot away, its tires squealing against the concrete drive.

She saw Curtis wince at the noise.

"What in heaven's name did he do?" she muttered, and rubbed her temple where a vein throbbed. "For the queen of self-control to lose it like that..."

Curtis shook his head. Glancing around to be sure the valet was no longer within ear-shot, he said, "I have to tell you, Ms. Kara—it's not like the old days."

"It's a whole lot more interesting, I'll bet. Though don't tell me the former members never pulled any stunts. They couldn't all be as straitlaced as my grandparents."

"But no matter what the old-time members did, they never lacked class," Curtis said earnestly. "Do you think it's really off?"

Kara tipped her head to one side. "What makes you ask that? She sounded pretty definite about it. I must ad-

mit I'd give a pretty penny to know exactly what the sun
king did to set her off, but—''

''Does it matter what he did?'' Curtis shrugged.

''Do you really think that if I cancel all the plans, by
next week I'll be scrambling to get everything back together? You might be right, you know. She was still wearing her diamond. She didn't throw it at him, which I'd
say is a pretty good sign.''

Curtis shifted his feet and didn't look at her.

Kara mused, ''Do you think that means he can talk her
around if he just puts his mind to it? An apology, a dozen
roses…''

*But what if he doesn't put his mind to it? Or what if
Jax Montgomery's offense—whatever it was—is serious
enough that an apology won't take care of it?*

For the first time, Kara faced the problem squarely.
Putting together a wedding the size of Anabel's was a
monumental challenge, but dismantling it would be worse
yet. For instance, what was she supposed to tell Rhonda,
surrounded by thirteen half-finished bridesmaids' dresses?
Rhonda, who had ordered a pricey bolt of lavender satin
that hadn't even come yet, and for which she would have
no earthly use now? Rhonda, who had not only cashed in
her baby's birth gifts to pay the rush charges, but who
still owed the supplier for the fabric itself?

If Kara broke the news to the caterer, the florist, the
photographer, the dance band and the seamstresses, re-
leasing them from their obligations, and then it turned out
that this was only a glitch in the plans—a mere misun-
derstanding—her carefully built reputation for unflappa-
ble organization would be torn to shreds. To say nothing
of how difficult it would be to reassemble the team.

But it would be even worse if she held back from telling everyone only to discover that Anabel's announce-

ment was firm. By delaying, she was eliminating any opportunity for the people Anabel had hired to find other jobs to fill the gap.

And she didn't have a snowball's chance of guessing which way it would end up. She knew Anabel fairly well, of course, after a few months of working with her. But Jax Montgomery was an absolute unknown. Would he even consider making an apology, or was he the stand-firm-no-matter-what type?

You still haven't even met the groom? Rhonda's concerned question rang through her mind once more, and Kara wanted to groan.

"I think," she said slowly, "it's time I scraped up an acquaintance with Mr. Montgomery."

Curtis obviously thought he'd said too much already for he didn't answer. Kara thought he seemed a bit reluctant as he opened the door for her.

The maître d' had returned to his stand outside the dining room, and he puffed up like a pigeon when Kara walked straight past him and started up the stairs. "You can't go up there," he announced.

Kara didn't pause or look over her shoulder. "Why not? Have the locker rooms been moved upstairs? If you're afraid I might be embarrassed..."

He gave a lofty sniff. "That area is for members only. And you're not a member, only an employee." He gave the word a twist that made it sound almost obscene.

Kara gritted her teeth for a second. "It's a member I'm going to see. I need a couple of minutes with Mr. Montgomery, to discuss his wedding. Remember? You'll be hosting it next month, right here." *Maybe.*

The maître d' relaxed slightly. "In that case, there's no need for you to go poking into private places. Mr.

Montgomery went out the back door a few minutes ago. I believe he was going to the driving range.''

Business as usual, Kara thought. The man was conducting himself just as if nothing had happened. A broken engagement was probably no more important on his calendar than a broken fingernail would be.

On the other hand, perhaps Jax Montgomery had dragged himself away from his harem—or whatever he'd been doing upstairs that had made Anabel so angry—to take out his frustration on a bucket of golf balls while he decided what to do about his erstwhile fiancée.

The trouble was, Kara thought, she wasn't sure whether that would be better news, or worse.

It had been years since she'd been on the Century Club's golf course, and then she'd merely been taking a few lessons—more to fill up the long days of a summer spent with her grandparents than because she was really interested in golf.

At the edge of the driving range, she paused to look for Jax Montgomery. She hadn't remembered the range being quite so large, but there were at least a dozen tees set up, at least a dozen men with buckets of golf balls, practicing their swings. All had their backs to her and most were wearing caps or visors. She didn't particularly want to walk up and down the line inspecting them till she found her quarry, but it looked as if she didn't have much choice.

At a nearby tee, a big man who was obviously the course professional looked over the shoulder of the golfer he was coaching and then came toward her, stopping directly in her path. Folding his powerful arms across his brightly striped shirt, he looked down at her. "Can I help you with something?" His tone said he doubted it.

"I'm looking for Jax Montgomery."

"If I see him, I'll give him the message."

While the pro hadn't exactly denied that Jax was there, it was apparent that he wouldn't come straight out and admit it, either —even if the man had been standing right next to him. Every employee of the Century Club learned the drill, Kara knew: the club was completely confidential, and no employee would admit to a stranger that any particular person was a member, much less that he was actually present. The pro was only doing his job, she reminded herself. Nevertheless, she felt her blood pressure rising.

"Now run along," he said gruffly. "You can't come out here."

"It's going to be a little tough for you to pass on a message, isn't it, since I haven't given you one?" Kara pointed out. "And just when did you stop letting women onto the course?"

"Properly clothed women can play anytime. But you can't wander around in those shoes."

She looked down at her low-heeled pumps and said flippantly, "Why not? All the golfers wear spikes."

He shook his head firmly. Kara shrugged and stepped out of her shoes. As she bent to pick them up, one of the golfers toward the far end of the row turned her way, and she recognized his profile. "You might want to have your eyes checked," she advised the pro, "because that's Jax Montgomery just over there." She ducked around him and padded across the carpet-smooth grass.

She'd seen pictures of Jax Montgomery, of course— hadn't everybody?—and also the society-page headlines that had called him and Anabel the most attractive couple in the city. But photographs hadn't prepared her for the man himself. It wasn't a matter of looks, though she found herself thinking that the chiseled cut of his profile showed up much better in person than in print. It certainly wasn't the way he was dressed in bright-colored, casual golf clothes like those of every other man on the driving range—though she had to admit that, unlike most of them, Jax didn't look as if he ought to be in the circus instead.

It was, she thought, the way he carried himself—with an air of assurance just a fraction short of arrogance— and the aura of power he projected. From six feet away, she could feel the energy field surrounding him, and the unexpectedness of it stopped her short. Despite the distance, the electricity he emitted made the hair on the back of her neck quiver, and it seemed to interfere with her heartbeat, as well.

He finished teeing up his ball, and as he straightened, his gaze flicked casually over her, lingering for a moment on her stocking-clad toes. He looked, she thought, just a little puzzled—as well he might.

She hadn't expected him to be so tall; even the statuesque Anabel wouldn't have to consider the height of her heels, and Kara—a good six inches shorter than the beauty queen—felt tiny and fragile next to him.

Of course, having shoes on would help, she reminded herself.

His gaze met hers, and sudden queasiness swept over her as she recognized the sharp calculation in his dark eyes. This was not going to be an easy man to talk to, but then, had she expected anything else?

His brief inspection over, Jax nodded silently at her and took his stance, gloved hands gripping the shaft of a driver. Kara took a couple of steps back and almost tripped over his bag of clubs—which had probably cost, she thought, roughly the same as her car.

She watched the muscles flex easily in his shoulders and his arms as he drove the ball long and straight down the range. He stood and watched it, and she watched him, noting the tiny lines around his eyes—narrowed, despite the visor he wore, to follow the ball's flight—and the way his dark hair curved near his ears. She'd bet that when he stepped out of a shower his hair would be a mass of ringlets. In fact, she could almost *see*...

But no matter how interesting the speculation, she couldn't run away from the job at hand. With an effort, she pulled herself back to the driving range. "Mr. Montgomery?" Her voice held a little-girl breathlessness that made her want to swear; how could she possibly feel so short of oxygen when she was surrounded by fresh air?

He looked at her again, more closely this time, and one dark eyebrow quirked upward.

"I'm Kara Schuyler. Your..." She hesitated. "The wedding planner."

His gaze flicked down across her plain navy blue dress to her shoeless feet, and his voice took on a tinge of irony. "Oh, yes—the arbiter of etiquette and high fashion. You have my sympathies—now that you're out of a job." He reached down for another ball from the bucket at his feet.

"Is that absolutely firm?"

"Didn't Anabel manage to convince you?" His voice was dry. "From what I heard as I was passing through the lobby, she seemed to be making herself fairly clear to everyone within three blocks. I don't see what I can possibly add to the discussion."

Kara wouldn't have been surprised if he'd laughed off Anabel's outburst. A great many men, she suspected, would have done exactly that—simply refused to believe what she was saying, expecting that with firmness and a bit of time the little woman would come around to the man's way of thinking.

The fact that Jax Montgomery appeared to be suffering

no illusions about his ex-fiancée's feelings indicated that he knew quite well the enormity of what he'd done, and it made Kara speculate once more about precisely what Anabel had seen in that upstairs room. Frankly, Kara thought, even a harem didn't seem quite extreme enough....

Obviously, she told herself, *my imagination needs a workout if I can't come up with anything more shocking than that!*

Jax was looking impatient, she realized, undoubtedly eager to get back to his practice. She had about fifteen more seconds to make her point—if that.

"It was apparent that Miss Randall's feelings are very strong," Kara said quickly. "And of course I took her seriously—up to a point. But surely you understand that most couples have a disagreement or two just before the wedding. Of course, everyone suffers from nerves..."

Except, she realized abruptly, Jax Montgomery didn't look like he possessed a single nerve to suffer from. Or at least, he hadn't until she'd started talking. Now he appeared to have developed a couple, and it was quite clear that Kara had managed to rub them both the wrong way.

"A disagreement," he said flatly.

It was too late to back out now, Kara knew. "Well, yes," she said carefully. "There's a great deal of stress at this time, only a couple of weeks before the wedding, and it's not at all unusual for a couple to have a..." She paused, looking for just the right word, one that would neither inflate the importance of a quarrel nor make light of it.

"A tiff?" he suggested.

Kara nodded, relieved to hear the calmer note in his voice. "It's almost universal, in fact. The strain of the wedding preparations..."

The words sounded hollow, even to her own ears. Jax Montgomery certainly wasn't suffering from the strain of wedding preparations; so far as Kara could see, he hadn't done a thing. She'd learned he hadn't even selected his bride's diamond, for Anabel had confided that she'd chosen the engagement ring herself. And the whole point of hiring a professional wedding planner was to relieve Anabel of as much of the stress and bother as possible. If there ever was a couple who could manage to avoid the last-minute stresses, it should be this one.

Jax hadn't missed the implications, of course. "You might want to abandon that line of argument, Ms. Schuyler," he advised. "It's going to be a tough sell to convince me that overwork is the gremlin here, either for Anabel or me."

"Even so, getting ready for a wedding still puts a strain on everyone," she said stubbornly. "Then naturally, there's a certain amount of anxiety and apprehension about the big changes that marriage will bring—"

"Changes," Jax said deliberately. "You mean things like living together? Sleeping together? Is that the sort of…changes you're talking about?"

The insinuation was clear, and Kara felt embarrassed color wash over her face. "Look, I don't care what the two of you have been doing," she snapped. "Marriage is still a big deal, and only an idiot isn't just a bit scared of the enormity of it. My point is, it's not at all unusual for a couple to let a minor disagreement get out of hand—"

"And break off an engagement?" He sounded disbelieving.

"You'd be surprised how often it happens. But outsiders usually don't know about it because the couple almost always patches things up. If one of them will just take the first step to break the ice—"

"You're suggesting I should apologize." It was not a question.

"It didn't appear that Ms. Randall had anything to apologize for," Kara said pointedly.

Jax considered that, then shook his head. "No, I doubt she'd consider it."

"So if the quarrel was your fault—"

"I thought you were a wedding planner, not some kind of shrink." He reached down to pick up a tee. "Now, if you don't mind…"

Kara stood her ground. "It doesn't take a counselor to see what's going on here. It's a shame to see it all go up in smoke."

"All your hard work, you mean?"

"All your high hopes," Kara said firmly. She felt pretty pompous, and it was apparent from the glitter in Jax Montgomery's eyes that he couldn't agree more. "And all the hard work, too, of course," she admitted. "I'd hate to see it wasted."

"What's the big deal? You get paid no matter what, don't you?"

"Not my full fee—but that's not my concern."

"Oh, I see. You can't tell everybody you're the genius behind the Montgomery wedding if it doesn't come off after all. So in order to save your professional reputation, I'm supposed to—"

Kara cut across him. "It's not that, either. I have plenty of references already. It's the others who are working on the wedding that I'm worried about. People have given up other jobs to take on this one, you know, and now if the wedding's canceled—"

"They'll have an unexpected free day."

"And they'll lose a great deal in the process. Take the photographer, for instance. There's a provision in his contract for a partial fee if the job is called off, of course, but he counts on extra sales of the pictures to make his real profit. If there's no wedding—''

"That means no pictures to sell." Jax shrugged. "I see your point, but I think you should be having this conversation with Anabel, not me. I didn't sign any contracts, and I don't owe anybody anything."

"I realize that, of course, but I thought—''

"Not that I expect it'll do you much good to talk to her."

"She didn't seem eager to carry out her responsibilities," Kara admitted. "But—''

"Not surprising since it was my money she was using." He raised his eyebrows. "What's the matter? Where did you think she was getting the cash?"

It had never occurred to Kara to ask herself that question. Anabel had never hesitated to commit the necessary amounts to get precisely what she wanted, and she'd never balked at writing the check when the bill arrived. Furthermore, she'd never uttered a murmur about needing anyone else's approval before making a decision.

From all appearances, she'd been completely at ease with wealth. But then, she was a beauty queen who'd been groomed to perfection in behavior as well as looks. What had seemed to be nonchalance where money was concerned could have simply been part of the performance—along with her designer clothes and expensive shoes and the easy way she signed her name to Century Club luncheon tabs....

Only now did Kara wonder if it had been her own name Anabel was signing, or Jax's.

If anyone should know better than to judge by appearances, Kara thought, *it's you. What a fool you are not to have remembered that.*

But if Anabel didn't have any money—which seemed to be what Jax Montgomery was saying—the contract she'd signed was worth little more than the paper it was written on.

And since Jax had signed nothing at all…

She took a deep breath and regrouped. "Technically you may not be obligated to pay the bills, Mr. Montgomery. But it's your wedding, too—"

"Not anymore," he said coolly.

"And it's your reputation on the line as well as Ms. Randall's. Your image as a gentleman, as an upright man of integrity—"

"Perhaps the word you're looking for is *patsy*."

Desperation made her clumsy, and before Kara could stop herself, the words burst out. "What does it matter? It's only money. That kind of pocket change means nothing to you…"

She watched his dark eyes turn to ice and knew she had just made the biggest mistake of her life.

"I suggest," Jax Montgomery said icily, "that you mind your own business and get down to work canceling a wedding."

He turned his back on her and stooped to tee up the ball he'd been holding. With barely a glance to make sure she was out of the way, he took a swing—not easy and relaxed this time, but savagely graceful—and with a whack that hurt Kara's ears, the golf ball soared out across the range.

Defeated, she stumbled off the driving range, not even remembering to put on her shoes till she'd reached her car and realized that the concrete parking lot had shredded her nylon stockings. She sat behind the wheel contemplating the runs in her hose and trying not to think about the just-as-thorough destruction of her business.

She had no doubt that Jax had told her the truth. It hadn't been Anabel's money she was spending in the first place, so it was no wonder the woman had announced that she wouldn't throw another penny down the drain. And if Anabel didn't have any resources, it would be a waste of time even to try to get her to live up to her contract.

What was she going to tell people like Rhonda? That she was awfully sorry, but nobody was going to reimburse her for that special-order bolt of lavender satin after all? That baby Dylan wasn't going to get his gift money back?

Kara could almost see her world tumbling down around her. In the three years it had taken to build her business, she'd made it a point to work with the best people available. But now the photographers, florists, caterers and dressmakers she'd so carefully cultivated would be the ones to take the hit, and they'd have trouble trusting her again. This could be the end of her business.

And the cost wouldn't only be professional since Rhonda wasn't the only friend she had among the people she worked with.

The fabric supplier's special-order charges had not only shocked Rhonda, they'd made Kara blanch; while she could repay Rhonda, it would leave Kara's budget hurting. In any case, it was hardly fair to help out one of her suppliers while ignoring the rest. The fact was that if she multiplied Rhonda's shortfall by the number of people who stood to lose money in this fiasco, Kara couldn't possibly make it up to them all.

Which brought her squarely back to Jax.

What she had said to him about pocket change might have been unwise, but it was true. The costs that would impoverish Kara would be peanuts to Jax Montgomery, the king of solar energy.

He might not technically be responsible for debts his ex-fiancée had taken on, but surely he bore a moral obligation. If Kara could just make him see the effects that his refusal to help would have on ordinary people—people like Rhonda, and Mrs. Gleason who was probably at this moment sewing crystal beads on Anabel's wedding gown...

Just remembering the price of those beads made Kara cringe. And it was no comfort to remember that she'd tried to convince Mrs. Gleason to change her policy and ask for a larger deposit up front—for Mrs. Gleason hadn't done it. And while Rhonda's loss would be serious, Mrs. Gleason's would be disastrous.

But convincing him was not going to be easy. *For that matter*, Kara thought, *if I even see him again, it'll only be because he didn't spot me first!*

She rolled her head from side to side, trying to ease the stiffness in her neck muscles. From the corner of her eye, she caught a glimpse of movement near her car and turned to get a better look.

Jax was coming across the parking lot, toward her car.

Hope flared inside her. Maybe he'd had second thoughts when he had a chance to consider what she'd said. If he was coming to talk to her about it...

She hastily slid out of her car so she could greet him properly, and in the process kicked her handbag out onto the concrete. *Great move, Schuyler*, she told herself as she stooped to pick up her things, cramming them back into the bag at random.

Breathless, with the last of her possessions still clutched in her hand, she stood up—and realized that he wasn't coming to see her at all. He was headed for a dark blue Jaguar parked nearby.

Kara could actually feel herself deflate. Then she swallowed hard and gritted her teeth. Surely it was worth one more try.

He was just opening the door as she followed him up to the vehicle. He'd changed into dark trousers and a crisp white shirt, and his still-damp hair was just as curly as she'd expected it would be. "Mr. Montgomery, if I could have just one more minute..."

He didn't even look at her. "This discussion is finished."

Kara glanced down at the penlight clutched so tightly in her hand that her fingers trembled. Without conscious consideration of what she was doing, she raised the tiny flashlight and jabbed the lens end hard into the small of his back.

Jax jerked upright. "What the hell... What's this? A gun?"

"How perceptive you are," she said coolly. "And to answer your next question—yes, it means I'm kidnapping you."

choice. "Besides, since there seems to be nobody within
range to hear, Jax, I might just as well shoot now."
"No," he gasped. "Maybe you should reload your Luger or
something reaction. Just a few bonus points."
"If I ever met a man who needed to have one good thing
about the way she was holding him," she thought. He knew

CHAPTER TWO

Jax twisted his head in a futile effort to see over his
shoulder. What kind of stunt was this screwball woman
trying to pull off anyway? Putting a gun to his back...if
it really was a gun, of course; he'd put the odds at about
four to one against. On the other hand, these days you
just never knew. Sometimes the strangest people turned
out to be the ones who were packing concealed weapons.

Which actually was no comfort at all—since Kara
Schuyler was shaping up to be the strangest woman he'd
run into in a good long time.

"Stand still," she ordered, and the object—whatever it
was—jabbed harder into his back.

"You've already got my attention," Jax protested.
"And if that really is a gun you're holding on me—"

"What makes you think it might not be?" She sounded
perfectly calm.

Not a good sign, he thought. If she was bluffing, he'd
expect to hear a flicker of doubt in her voice, but there
was none. "Then stop acting as if it's a knife," he finished. "It isn't going to do you any good to try to stab
me with a gun barrel."

"Oh." The pressure eased slightly. "If you're thinking
of yelling for help, I wouldn't suggest it. Or are you too
macho to want anybody to know you're in a jam?"

"It *would* ruin my image, you know," he said earnestly. He leaned forward a bit, bracing his hands on the
Jaguar's door. It went very much against the grain to kick
a woman, but Kara Schuyler wasn't offering him much

choice. "Besides, since there seems to be nobody within range to hear me, it appears to be a moot point."

"Exactly. Maybe you should rethink your policy on self-protection. Hire a few bodyguards."

"I'll bear that in mind." There was one good thing about the way she was poking him, Jax thought. He knew exactly where her hand was. If every few seconds he could shift his feet a bit and at the same time turn a fraction of an inch, he might get himself into position to whirl around, grab her arm and break her grip before she could react. He kept talking, trying to distract her so he could move. "Well, what are we going to do next? It's immense fun just to stand here with you, of course, but—"

"There's somebody I want you to talk to."

Jax almost forgot the pressure against his back. "Look, sweetheart, if you're of the opinion that getting Anabel and me together for a heart-to-heart will be enough to solve this crisis—"

"It's not Anabel I'm taking you to see. If you want to talk to her, that's your business. I've decided it's none of my affair. Get in the car."

He hesitated, and she prodded him once more. Was it just his imagination, or could he actually feel the coldness of steel through the crisp white shirt? This was getting downright serious.

"Excuse me," he said gently, easing another inch into his turn, "but I see a little practical difficulty arising here. I assume—since I don't know where I'm going or whom I'm meeting—that you intend to ride along?"

"Of course I'm going. What kind of idiotic question is that?"

"You understand, of course, that my experience with kidnapping comes mostly from the movies," he said. *And*

I'll bet yours does, too. "But I can't quite get the logistics clear in my mind. If I'm sitting behind the wheel, where are you going to be? In the passenger seat? And exactly how do you plan to keep me under control while you walk around the front of the car and open the door? Or are you going to get in first and give me the chance to run while you're getting settled?"

She hesitated for only an instant. "Easy. You get in, slide across into the passenger seat—and I'll drive."

"Now *that* idea I find even more terrifying than the gun. Tell you what, Kara darling. Let's make a deal. You have somebody you want me to talk to. All right, I'll talk. You don't have to hold me hostage."

The pressure on his back wavered just a trifle. "You mean that?"

"My word of honor as a gentleman. What was it you called me? An upright man of integrity?"

"I'd almost rather you swore an oath as a patsy." She sounded reluctant. "What are you up to anyway?"

"Nothing." He held up a hand as if he were taking a Boy Scout pledge. "It just occurred to me that your trying to handle both a gun and an unfamiliar vehicle in busy traffic could end up being pretty messy for not only me but my car."

"You're worried about a car? I thought you'd have at least ten Jaguars."

"This is my favorite one. Do we have a deal?"

She didn't answer but took half a step back, and the pressure on his back vanished. He'd probably carry the indentation for life, Jax thought.

Slowly, he moved away from the door, leaving room for her to pass. "After you, my dear...oh, and put that thing away, would you? I'd hate to have you shoot yourself in the foot with a flashlight."

Her astonished gasp made him want to howl with laughter. "You knew? How? When?"

He turned to face her and leaned against the door, grinning. "I caught a glimpse of your hand in the mirror about a minute ago. And since I've never seen anybody hold a gun in a grip like yours, I took a second look."

Her shoulders sagged. Suddenly, she seemed to be the least threatening creature on the face of the earth. Her small pointed chin trembled, and her eyes—deep green, he thought—brimmed with tears.

Her voice was bitter. "I can't do anything right, can I? I'm not one inch further along—"

"Of course you are. I said I'd go with you, didn't I?"

Her eyes *were* green—the dark shade of a still, deep pool of lake water—and very wide. "You'll actually keep your word?"

"Just call me a patsy," he said cheerfully. "Now, are we going or not?"

She didn't bother to answer, just scrambled into the car. As she slid across the seat, her navy blue skirt rode up a whole lot higher than it had ever been intended to go, showing off a nicely shaped knee and a lusciously slender thigh.

So the prim exterior is only wrapping paper, Jax thought, And darned if Kara Schuyler wasn't beginning to look like a package that might be a great deal of fun to unwrap.

Kara's ears were still buzzing with the aftereffects of her audacity—and the slick way he'd disarmed her—when the Jaguar paused at the end of the Century Club's long driveway.

It was just as well that things had turned out as they had, she concluded. She'd been shaking so much she'd have been hard-pressed to maintain the illusion of a steady trigger finger for much longer anyway.

"Which way?" Jax asked.

"Toward downtown."

The Jaguar made a smooth turn onto the main street and a couple of minutes later swooped onto the freeway. As soon as the car had merged smoothly into traffic, Jax shot a look across at her. "Just as a matter of curiosity, why aren't you dragging me over to see Anabel? If you're so certain this is just a spat—"

"Because you're obviously convinced it isn't—and you should know. So why waste the time?"

Kara didn't know herself exactly when she'd reached the conclusion that no matter what else occurred, the Montgomery-Randall wedding was not going to take place as scheduled. She didn't even quite know why she was suddenly so certain because everything she'd said to him out on the driving range was still just as true.

Every couple had last-minute doubts. Almost every couple had a zinger of a fight in the few weeks before the wedding. A goodly portion of them threatened to call off the ceremony, and still almost every one of those couples ended up married anyway.

But somewhere along the line, Kara had stopped believing in the percentages—at least where this couple was concerned.

Curiosity got the better of her. "Exactly what did you do that upset Anabel enough to walk out on all your money—to say nothing of your sterling self?"

He turned to glance at her, his gaze level and cool.

The odd queasiness that Kara had felt on the driving range, the first time she'd met his eyes, rushed over her again. She swallowed hard. "Never mind. Forget I asked," she said hastily.

"You're certain you don't want to know?" He sounded perfectly calm, and yet there was something about his tone that warned her to be careful. "All those people you have to cancel might ask questions."

"Right now, my only goal is to get out of this mess with the least painful consequences for everyone." *Just how stuffy can you sound? she asked herself.*

"Except for me, perhaps," Jax said.

Kara bit her lip. Perhaps some fence-mending was in order.

"Mr. Montgomery…" she began tentatively.

"Oh, I think sticking me up is enough of an introduction for us to use first names. So whom are you taking me to see, Kara?"

"I'd rather not tell you till we get there."

"Aha—a woman of mystery. I understand. How'd you get into the wedding business?"

Kara didn't fool herself into thinking that he really cared. He was no doubt playing by the psychology book, attempting to befriend his kidnapper. Wasn't that what one was supposed to do when in a hostage situation— build bridges and cement the human contact in the hope of talking oneself out of the difficulty?

Not that he hadn't already done a pretty fair job of getting himself off the hook, Kara reflected. He could easily have left her there and driven off, laughing. But he hadn't; he'd held to his word. The least she could do in return was make civil conversation.

He glanced over at her again. "Personal experience?"

"In a way. I've never been married, but I'd collected so much experience from being a bridesmaid that I started helping all my friends with their plans, and it just kind of grew."

"And there are enough weddings to keep you busy?"

"I'm as busy as I want to be. I do all kinds of parties, actually—anniversaries, housewarmings, corporate receptions. On Saturday, I'm making a pitch to do all of Donald Sloan's entertaining."

"The razor tycoon? He's such a recluse I'm surprised he's even talking to you."

"His daughter is turning sixteen, so they're having a party. Girls used to have debuts. Now they have sweet-sixteen celebrations. It's not my favorite sort of event, but if the Sloans like what I do with it—well, there's something to be said for regular clients."

"Just don't expect one of them to be Donald Sloan," Jax recommended. "Where's he meeting you?"

"I'm going to the house."

He gave a low whistle. "You *are* a heavy hitter," he murmured. "Anabel said something about your knowing everybody who counts in society."

"Let's just say I know who used to be married to whom so they don't get seated at the same table." She caught sight of a street sign and abruptly leaned forward. "Here—take the next exit and turn left at the light."

Before long, they were on a quiet street of brownstones, most of which had been converted into apartments, one per floor. Kara pointed out a parking spot.

"I'd really like to know just a little about this person you're so determined I meet," he said.

"I'm sure you would." Kara led the way up the stairs and rang Mrs. Gleason's doorbell.

A quavery voice called, "It's open."

Kara grimaced and turned the knob. "I'd feel much better if you'd lock this, Mrs. Gleason," she said.

A tiny white-haired woman with faded blue eyes looked up from the wedding veil that lay across her lap, lace edging partially in place. "And put down my sewing every time someone knocks? My dear, what a lovely surprise to see you today. And you've brought..." She paused to give Jax the once-over. "My goodness."

She sounded almost coy. Kara smothered a sigh. Was the man deadly to women of all ages? She introduced them, but instead of listening to Jax charm Mrs. Gleason, she glanced around the room and hoped he would display more than the average male's powers of observation. It would be far more effective if he saw the worn spots in the carpet and felt the rickety springs in the couch himself rather than have them pointed out to him.

"I brought Mr. Montgomery," she explained, "so he could see all the work you've done on Miss Randall's wedding dress. He's a great lover of beauty, and I know he'll appreciate seeing your workmanship."

Mrs. Gleason frowned. "But, Kara dear, that style would be all wrong for you. You're far too slim and boyish for that silhouette."

Kara blinked in astonishment at the non sequitur. Had the woman lost her mind?

Before Kara could find her voice, Mrs. Gleason went straight on. "I think a Roaring Twenties sort of style would be perfect for you. You know what I mean, something like that dinner dress I made for you last winter. A nice, straight line from the shoulders down, trimmed with fringe and beads."

Jax took a step back and tipped his head to one side to study Kara from head to toe. His face was impassive, but his eyes glinted as he slowly made his survey.

Kara wanted to scream. He'd looked her over pretty thoroughly on the driving range; what else was there to see?

"You're right, Mrs. Gleason," he said. "That's precisely what she needs. With an extremely short skirt to show off those incredible legs..."

Of course, Kara thought. *Compared to a Miss World finalist, I'm pretty incredible all right.* When he leaned down, hand outstretched as if to run it along her leg—as if, Kara decided irritably, he was showing off a pony!— she started to do a slow burn. "Knock it off, Montgomery."

"But I'm only making myself agreeable. You did bring me to meet the lady, so I assumed you'd want me to—"

"Kara, what happened to you?" Mrs. Gleason sounded horrified. "Your stockings are in shreds!"

"Just a little accident, Mrs. Gleason. If we could look at Miss Randall's dress...?"

"But it's nothing like I'd make for you," the older woman protested. "It's not only that the style's wrong, but even the color...You can't wear white, you know. Why don't you let me get a notebook and sketch a few ideas for you?"

"She can't wear white?" Jax's eyes had widened, and his voice trembled in the best imitation of shock Kara had ever seen. "I'm stunned. I had no idea..." He raised an eyebrow at Kara and said in his normal tone, "Is that disagreeable enough to satisfy you? Or would you like me to beat Mrs. Gleason up for implying that you're not a virgin?"

Kara opened her mouth only to find that she didn't have anything to say. And it would hardly be prudent right now, she told herself firmly, to give Jax the punch in the jaw that he so richly deserved.

Mrs. Gleason dimpled up at him. "You needn't be dismayed, young man. I only meant Kara's dress will have to be ivory instead of pure white. It means exactly the same thing, but it would be much better for her coloring, don't you think?''

''Oh,'' Jax said with a long sigh of obviously feigned relief. ''I'm glad you cleared that up.''

''Blondes have to be so careful about white,'' the woman pointed out.

Kara took a deep breath and tried again. ''Mrs. Gleason, I'm afraid you have the wrong—''

''But isn't that why you're here? To choose your wedding gown? Though you really shouldn't have brought the groom, dear. He shouldn't even know about your dress till you walk down the aisle—''

''Mrs. Gleason.'' Kara raised her voice. ''We are not a couple. I'd like Mr. Montgomery to see all the work you've done on Miss Randall's dress.''

''But why? If you're not... Oh.'' Mrs. Gleason looked distressed. ''You're *that* Mr. Montgomery? But you really shouldn't have even a glimpse—''

''Mrs. Gleason,'' Kara said firmly. ''*Get the dress*.''

The woman blinked in hurt surprise, but without a word she retreated toward a closed door at the far side of the living room.

''If this is how you treat the people you work with...'' Jax began.

''Don't start on me. I'm not being rude for the fun of it, you know. I just don't want to tell her the wedding's off until I can also tell her that she's not going to lose money on the deal. That's why I brought you here—because I want you to observe how much time and effort Mrs. Gleason's invested in this gown. After you've seen it, I'll tell you about the down payment Anabel made—and I'm sure you'll be able to do the math. Then if you'll look around and see how much Mrs. Gleason needs every penny—''

"Careless of you, not to arrange things better than that."

"Technically, I'm just the go-between. Every person involved in a wedding sets his own rules on getting paid. I put together the right team and supervise, make sure everything fits together on the day."

"So why do you feel so responsible?"

"Because I'm the one who got them involved in the first place. What's the big deal anyway? If Anabel had paid the whole amount up front, it would have been with your money, and surely you don't think you'd be due a refund now?"

"You actually want me to pay for a wedding gown I have absolutely no use for?"

Kara wrinkled her nose. "Are you certain you'll never need it? It might be handy to have one already hanging in the closet in case you decide to get married on the spur of the moment someday."

"Oh, with my luck, she won't be able to wear white."

"What a surprise that would be," Kara muttered. "So call me up when it happens and I'll dye the damned thing red. Though come to think of it, if Anabel was going to try to pass for pure, why couldn't the next one, too?"

His eyes began to sparkle, but before he could speak, Mrs. Gleason reappeared, her arms loaded with white satin. She hung Anabel's dress from a low hook near her small rocking chair, letting the white satin skirt and attached train puff out over the carpet. Sunlight fell across the glossy fabric and caught at each surface of the thousands of iridescent beads that formed rose motifs at seemingly random patterns over the skirt.

On a low table beside the chair was a saucer full of crystal beads waiting to be applied, and just visible in one of the folds of satin were the half-dozen fine needles Mrs. Gleason had been using to attach yet another rose motif.

"There," the woman said. She actually dusted her hands together as if dismissing all responsibility for whatever calamity arose from letting the groom see the dress before the proper time. "Perhaps, while you look, I'll go make some tea."

"That would be wonderful, Mrs. Gleason," Kara said warmly. "If you don't mind, we'll just sit here on the couch and admire your work."

She perched on the edge of the cushion. Jax sat down next to her; from the corner of her eye, she saw him wince and wanted to laugh. But he didn't complain, only leaned forward to study the pool of satin. "Looks like a waste of good material to me."

"Especially for someone as skinny as Anabel." She said it deliberately, wondering if Jax would spring to the beauty queen's defense.

He shot a sideways glance at her and returned to his inspection. "Why don't you like Anabel?"

"I never said I didn't. In any case, I don't have to like my clients to do a good job for them."

"Oh, it's all right to admit it. She doesn't think a lot of you, either—though it's clear she never met up with the real Kara Schuyler. Anabel told me you were so prim and proper you probably wear white gloves to bed. I wonder what she'd have said if she'd seen the holdup. So what's next?"

Kara said carefully, "Then you agree to take care of Mrs. Gleason's losses?"

"I haven't agreed to anything. I simply meant the wedding gown can't be the end of it."

"No, it isn't. I believe I've already mentioned the photographer? Well, there's also the dance band, the woman who's making all the bridesmaids' dresses——''

''Wait a minute. Isn't that the bridesmaids' responsibility? I may not be the etiquette king of high society, but I know a few things, and you're not pulling that one over on me.''

''Technically, you're right. But you don't really suppose that Anabel's friends are going to want those dresses, under the circumstances, do you?''

''They look that bad, huh?''

''Of course they don't. They're beautiful, and Rhonda's workmanship is superb. But how many young women really have a need for a purple ball gown, or six hundred dollars to invest in one that will hang in the closet and gather dust without having been worn even once? Believe me, they'll leap at the chance to abandon them.''

''Six hundred dollars a dress? Desertion sounds like a sensible choice to me.''

Kara went on firmly, ''Then there's the cake—or shall I say cakes? Anabel asked for a special-order champagne fountain built in between the layers and a handmade china ornament for the top decoration. And the florist told me just last week he'd already put in the order for her orchids—so many of them that his supplier thought he must have mixed up the numbers.''

Jax nodded thoughtfully. ''Things are going to be tough for a lot of people, aren't they?''

Kara relaxed a trifle. Ill-planned as her demonstration had been, it was working, after all; he was getting the message, and surely his own sense of fair play would do the rest. ''That's the entire point,'' she said. ''All these people have agreed to provide a service, and it's not their fault if you—and Anabel, of course—suddenly decide you don't want their professional expertise after all. They shouldn't be penalized for doing their best.''

''Come to think of it, the only supplier you don't sound concerned about is the Century Club.''

''I haven't gotten around to them yet—or the caterer or the judge or—''

''The judge is my great-uncle. You don't have to worry about him.''

''What a relief. And believe me, the Century Club doesn't need my help to get its share, either. The manager will probably just add the shortfall to your dues.''

Mrs. Gleason came back with a laden tray, and Jax leaped up to take it from her. No doubt, Kara thought, he was glad of the excuse to remove himself from the uncomfortable couch. When he sat down again, she noted with amusement, it was in a straight chair nearby.

Mrs. Gleason seemed to have gotten over her displeasure and didn't even cast a glance toward the dress. *Maybe she's just pretending it's not there because then the groom can't have seen it and jinxed the wedding*, Kara thought. *If she only knew…*

Kara helped herself to the assortment of tiny sandwiches and made a mental note to bring replacement goodies on her next visit. She disposed of a tiny chicken salad sandwich in two bites and reached for another. She noticed Jax watching her and said testily, ''Sorry to offend you with my appetite. Perhaps you didn't know I was supposed to have lunch with Anabel today—until you so rudely brought things to a halt.''

''I wasn't offended. Just interested to see a woman eating with such…gusto.''

Very deliberately, Kara polished off the sandwich. ''You're undoubtedly used to Anabel. It's no wonder she keeps that incredible figure—the woman never eats anything.''

"She will right before the wedding," Mrs. Gleason predicted. "So I've left a little room for letting the seams out. Don't forget to remind her about the last-minute fittings, Kara."

Kara took another bite so she could nod instead of giving a real answer. She eyed Jax. "So how about it?" she hinted.

He reached toward the tray without looking at her. "How about what? The cream puffs? That was the best one I've tasted in ages, Mrs. Gleason."

Mrs. Gleason beamed and urged him to have another.

Kara glared at him. He ignored her.

It was half an hour longer before she could get to her feet, thank Mrs. Gleason for the tea and the style show and get Jax out the door—and then he was carrying a paper plate full of leftover goodies. "Charming woman," he said as they walked back to his car. "I'm delighted you took me to meet her." He opened Kara's door for her.

"And, of course, the cream puffs. How about getting to the point, Montgomery?"

"Which point? There's no doubt that Anabel's got things in a mess, if that's what you mean. There's also no doubt that it's not up to me to fix it." He closed her door with a gentle click which was somehow more final than a slam.

She waited till he'd carefully set the loaded plate on the back seat and slid behind the wheel. "There's a difference between what's legal and what's moral," she argued. "I'm not legally accountable, either, but I feel a moral obligation to help."

"So go right ahead and do it," he suggested gently.

"You said yourself it's only money. If you're so concerned about these people, why don't you take care of them?"

She had no one to blame but herself, Kara knew. She'd unknowingly set the trap and then walked straight into it.

"Believe me," she said bitterly, "I wish I'd never bothered to come out to the golf course to find you."

He started the Jaguar and pulled out into the street. "I have no doubt of that, Kara Josephine."

"If I could afford the bills, I'd—" Abruptly, the name registered. "What did you call me? My grandmother was the only one who—"

He cut across Kara and two lanes of traffic simultaneously, heading up the ramp onto the freeway. "Don't expect me to believe that the Schuyler fortune can't afford this. You're the one who called it pocket change, you know."

"I said it would be pocket change for..."

She paused and stared at him—at the hard line of his throat, the fine lines around his eyes, the perfectly sculpted ear—and suddenly, her vision blurred and time seemed to shift. Suddenly, she knew why she'd felt so odd on the driving range when she'd first met his gaze. It hadn't been fear of the coming confrontation that had made her queasy. It had been subconscious recognition.

"They called you Jack back then," she whispered.

He didn't look at her. "Never could convince them of my proper name."

Kara hardly heard him; she was more than a decade in the past. "Back when you were working at the Century Club, caddying."

"And busing tables in the dining room—don't forget that part. And running errands for a whole lot of teenage girls who preferred to lounge around the pool and issue orders rather than walk across to the lemonade stand for themselves. Including a little snip of a thing called Kara Josephine Schuyler.''

Kara flung her head back against the Jaguar's soft leather seat. "And you're still carrying a grudge. No wonder—''

"I wouldn't call it a grudge, exactly. But being taken advantage of has never been my idea of good fun. Back then, I couldn't do much about it, but these days—''

"Look," Kara interrupted, "why don't you just let me off right here and we'll forget this ever happened?''

"What's the matter? Can't stand being in my presence unless you can issue orders?''

"No. I only meant…'' She sighed. "I thought, under the circumstances, there was no point in going on any longer. I know I'm not going to convince you of anything.''

"Probably true. But it would be a bit difficult to pick up a cab on the edge of the freeway. Besides, we're only half a dozen blocks from the club.'' He flicked the turn signal and shifted lanes. "Anyway, what did you mean when you said *if* you could afford the bills?''

She bit her lip. The last thing she wanted to do was satisfy Jax Montgomery's idle curiosity—and give him something else to gloat about. But she didn't have much of a choice. "The Schuyler fortune doesn't exist anymore.''

He didn't answer for a long moment and he didn't take his gaze off the street ahead. When he spoke, however, his tone was casual. "Ran through it that fast, did you?''

"Of course not," Kara snapped. "It was gone before I ever saw a penny.''

"Let me guess. Your father made a whole lot of bad investments.''

"I don't see that it matters where the money went, or how. It's gone."

"Oh, I'm just being nosy," he said cheerfully. "But I can't say I'm surprised. All those years ago, it was apparent that your grandfather didn't have a whole lot of faith in his son."

Kara stared at him. "Obviously, being nosy isn't a new talent for you."

The corner of his mouth quirked upward. "It's amazing how many people believe waiters and busboys and caddies are completely deaf or else subhuman and incapable of rational thought. They'll talk about darned near anything in front of the staff. It's as if those people weren't even there."

"Is that how you got your start? Listening in on businessmen's conversations?"

He glanced at her and smiled. "I picked up a stock tip or two along the way. Or are you accusing me of blackmail? Sorry to disappoint you. It's true, though, that I could have turned a tidy profit that way—even among the girls around the pool."

"It would've been interesting to see the payment plans they offered," Kara said tartly. The Jaguar turned into the Century Club's driveway and she reached down to get her handbag. "Well, it's been interesting, Jax, catching up on old times like this. If you'll just drop me beside my car—"

"You amaze me, Kara Jo. You're going to give up that easily? I thought you'd at least offer to take me into the lounge for a cup of coffee so you could keep talking."

"I'd have to sign your name to the check."

He didn't answer. The Jaguar slowed to a crawl as it neared the clubhouse, and she saw his eyes narrow.

Kara followed his gaze. Parked in front of the clubhouse were two police cruisers, their lights flashing. A nearby van, bristling with antennas and satellite relay dishes, displayed the splashy logo of the biggest television station in the city. On the portico, one of the cops, almost surrounded by people, was writing on a clipboard.

"What's going on?" Kara gasped.

Jax shot her a look. "Well, I doubt it's a fund-raiser for the care and feeding of elderly poodles. I'm betting that the parking lot wasn't quite as empty as we thought it was when you pulled the flashlight on me."

Kara could feel the blood draining from her face.

The cop with the clipboard looked up, said something to his partner, then started toward the Jaguar.

"Sit still and keep your hands in sight," Jax warned. "And pretend you don't know what's going on, all right?"

Kara was glad he hadn't told her to move because she didn't think she could. And as for playing dumb—well, that was no challenge at all.

He turned off the engine and slid out to stand beside the car, folding his arms across the top of the open door. His voice sounded carefully casual, but Kara could hear the strained note underneath. "What happened? Some-body get upset over a card game?"

"Mr. Montgomery?" one of the officers called.

"That's me. Is there a problem?"

A flash of red caught Kara's eye as Anabel darted from the Century Club's portico toward the Jaguar and flung herself full length against Jax, pushing him back against the car. "Darling," she whimpered, "thank heaven you're safe. I've lived a year since I got the news—"

"What news?" Jax sounded as if the impact had knocked the air out of him.

Or, Kara thought, as if the sheer unexpectedness of Anabel's response had snatched his breath away.

"That you'd been kidnapped. Oh, my darling, I'm so sorry, I've reconsidered everything."

Jax looked stunned.

Kara didn't know whether to laugh or cry. She'd solved the wedding crisis after all—she'd single-handedly achieved the impossible and bridged the rift between Jax and Anabel. The Montgomery wedding was back on schedule.

But she, it appeared, wouldn't be taking part because, in the process, she'd landed herself with a kidnapping charge.

Numbly, she watched as the second cop closed in on her.

CHAPTER THREE

THERE was, of course, only one thing he could do.

Just as the officer got into position beside Kara's door, Jax spoke up. "Kidnapped? That's nonsense, Anabel." Deliberately, he pitched his voice to carry across the parking lot. "Where on earth did you get that idea?"

Anabel glared up at him, but she didn't stop clinging. "Charley saw it happen. That's where I got the idea. I don't know why you're denying it, but..." She looked past him and gasped. "It was *her*? Miss White Gloves herself?"

"Now you understand why I said it's nonsense." Jax peeled Anabel's arms loose and turned around just as Kara obediently leaned against the Jaguar's side, hands flat against the gleaming surface. He hoped she wouldn't make any fast moves. Surely she had that much sense....

Though perhaps to credit Kara with common sense was taking the optimistic point of view, he reminded himself. That little circle in the small of his back still tingled whenever he thought about the flashlight stunt.

"Don't frown at *me*, Jax Montgomery," Kara said. "It isn't my idea to leave my fingerprints all over your favorite car. I'm only obeying orders. But I'll be very careful not to chip the paint."

Her voice was a little shaky, but she'd obviously picked up her cue.

Jax faced the cop who wasn't guarding Kara, the one who seemed to be in charge. "Sorry you've been put to all this trouble, officer. Nothing happened."

47

A young man stepped forward from the crowd near the portico. "But I saw it all, Mr. Montgomery," he said, and pointed at Kara. "I saw her standing behind you in the parking lot, holding something—"

"Holding something? So you decided she was a kidnapper?" This must be Charley, Jax deduced. Wasn't that what Anabel had called him? He vaguely remembered seeing the young man around the club, but he'd never known his name.

The young man swallowed hard, but he went on without a quiver; Jax had to admire his moxie. "And I saw you get into the car and drive off together—"

"Then you must have also seen me help her into the car," Jax pointed out.

One of the cops said dryly, "Mr. Montgomery, if you don't mind, *we'll* conduct this investigation."

I thought I was doing just fine, Jax thought. "There's not much to investigate. Do I look like I'm being held hostage?" He waved a careless hand at Kara. "Besides, why would a kidnapper calmly deliver the victim back to the scene of the crime?"

"But I saw—" Charley took a deep breath and shook his head as if to clear it. "Maybe I was wrong, but it sure looked like…"

The cop standing by Kara rolled his eyes and muttered something Jax couldn't quite hear. He thought it was probably just as well.

"Mr. Montgomery," the officer in charge said, "if you say there wasn't a kidnapping, there's nothing further we can do."

"Now you're making some sense."

"But before you decide you're not going to press charges, I'd like you to come into the clubhouse so we can talk about it in private."

"I wouldn't mind getting rid of the audience," Jax admitted, "but what charges would I press anyway? We went out for tea." Inspiration struck; he swung around to the car, opened the back door and triumphantly pulled out Mrs. Gleason's paper plate full of goodies. "Here's all the evidence you need."

"Nevertheless, we're all going inside," the officer declared.

"If you insist," Jax said. "But I'm not sharing the cream puffs. You'll have to take my word for how good they are."

"Along with taking your word for a lot of other things, it appears," the cop muttered.

Jax's heartbeat slowed a trifle. They weren't out of the woods yet, but he thought he could see the glimmer of sunlight in the distance.

If the officers took Jax's word for it...

Kara released a breath she didn't realize she'd been holding. She met the doubt-filled gaze of the officer nearest her and remembered abruptly that she was supposed to be an irritated innocent. "Do you mind if I get my handbag out of the car?" she asked sweetly. "I'd hate to leave it sitting here while we're all inside."

The cop was every bit as sarcastically polite. "Not if you don't mind me looking through it."

"How kind of you to ask before searching," she murmured.

They formed an odd little procession, Kara thought. First the young man who'd caused all the trouble, followed by Jax with Anabel clinging to his arm as if she'd been surgically attached, then Kara with her police shadow, and finally, the officer in charge bringing up the rear, clipboard once more in hand and Kara's purse slung across his shoulder.

The imperturbable Curtis held the door, then stepped firmly into the path of the television crew, blocking them from entering. That was one benefit of moving inside, Kara decided. The other bonus, in her opinion, was the expression on the face of the maître d' as he watched the invasion; he looked as if he'd swallowed a crab.

In the lounge, her escort guided her to a booth in the far corner overlooking the swimming pool, as far as possible from the table where the officer in charge had waved Jax to a seat. Anabel was still beside him, but as the minutes wore on, Kara could hear the beauty queen's toes tapping impatiently against the terrazzo floor.

Kara stared out at the sparkling water and thought about those long-ago encounters with Jax Montgomery. She couldn't remember specific incidents—as Jax so obviously could. The best she could do proved to be a few recollections so hazy she wasn't sure how much was actual memory and how much was guilty speculation. She probably had been the snip he'd called her. But then, wasn't every teenage girl a little over the top at times? And considering that she'd only come to the Century Club while she was visiting her grandparents, it was no wonder if she'd have been acting out every chance she got.

A tall glass of lemonade came to rest on the table in front of her, and the young man who had caused all the trouble said, "I thought the least I could do after all that was get you a drink. May I sit down?" He didn't wait for permission. "I'm really sorry, you know. As soon as Anabel said your name, I knew I must be wrong."

Kara raised her eyebrows. As best she could recall,

Anabel hadn't used her name. *Miss White Gloves herself*, she'd said.

"Anyway, you're not the kind of amazon it would take to force Jax Montgomery to do anything he didn't want to. He could break you in two with one hand, and I should've realized that from the beginning. All the trouble I've caused you..."

Guilt washed away Kara's annoyance. The poor man had been doing his civic duty; she couldn't let him abase himself any further, especially since he'd been absolutely correct. And yet, under the circumstances, she could hardly confess the truth, either. "I'm sure you did what you thought was right."

"That's very generous of you." He put out a hand. "My name's Charley Morgan. Maybe we could..."

The officer in charge crossed the room clutching Kara's purse. "Thanks for your patience, miss," he said dryly. "You're free to go now." He beckoned to his partner. "Come on, Joe, we're finished here."

Kara stood up. Her knees were a bit shaky, but otherwise she was all right.

"I'll walk you to your car," Charley Morgan offered eagerly.

She gave him an abstracted smile and looked thoughtfully across the room at Jax. Now that it was all over, she had to admit she'd like to know why he'd covered up for her. But right now was hardly the time to ask; he and Anabel were obviously absorbed in sorting out their differences. The only surprise about that, Kara observed, was that the beauty queen wasn't entwined around her once-more-beloved as if she never intended to let go.

There would be other chances to catch him alone for a moment, she told herself, in the two weeks that remained until his wedding day.

Two more interminable weeks. The time couldn't pass fast enough for Kara.

Under any other circumstances, Kara would have been delighted to see Rhonda on the front lawn shared by the two halves of the duplex, with baby Dylan asleep in his stroller and Cleo the Persian cat stalking a caterpillar nearby.

Today, however, Kara wasn't in the mood for company, even that of a best friend. *Especially* a best friend who was so intimately—even if unknowingly—involved in the day's events. She'd a whole lot rather Rhonda never knew how close all of them had come to disaster today.

But attempting to avoid Rhonda would only lead to questions, so Kara parked her car in the garage attached to her half of the duplex and walked out to the flower bed where Rhonda was pulling water grass from a bed of lilies.

Rhonda sat back on her heels. "What happened to the dull, matronly look? Your panty hose have so many holes it looks as if you've unraveled them on purpose just to make interesting patterns."

Kara had forgotten her shredded stockings. So much else had happened since she'd walked from the driving range across the parking lot carrying her shoes because she was too stunned by her first encounter with Jax Montgomery to stop and put them on. "It's the newest fad."

"I suppose next you'll tell me that Anabel taught you that trick." Rhonda turned back to her flowers. "I've got spaghetti sauce simmering if you'd like to come for dinner."

"Thanks. It sounds good, but I'm really tired. I'm just going to take it easy tonight."

Rhonda's eyebrows rose. "It's not even five o'clock in the afternoon, Kara. What have you been doing to—never mind, I can see you don't want to tell me. Go have a nap and you might change your mind about dinner." She shifted her position to reach the other end of the flower bed, and her eyes widened as she looked past Kara toward the street. "On the other hand," she murmured, "I won't be a bit surprised to find that you prefer this to spaghetti. If he's your definition of taking it easy, Kara…"

Kara twisted around.

The dark blue Jaguar was parked at the curb, and Jax was crossing the lawn toward them, his unhurried stride covering the ground at a remarkable pace.

What now? Kara wondered. She could think of a half-dozen reasons he might have come—none of which she found particularly reassuring. "This is a surprise."

"Is it really?" He turned his smile on Rhonda and held out a hand. "Jackson Montgomery. Sorry to interrupt, but I looked away for a second and Kara disappeared, so I came to find her."

Rhonda's eyes had widened, but she didn't miss a beat. "You have to keep an eye on her all the time," she confided. "Kara's just full of surprises."

Jax's eyes gleamed. "I've discovered that."

"I suppose," Kara said, "that you're here to make me buff out the fingerprints I left on your car."

He stooped to hold out a hand to Rhonda's cat, and to Kara's utter astonishment, the animal rubbed against his wrist and started to purr. "Oh, no, I intend to keep them as a souvenir of our unforgettable afternoon. I just stopped by for…coffee." The glint in his eyes suggested differently.

Rhonda choked.

Kara gritted her teeth. It was apparent Jax would say

whatever was on his mind no matter the audience—and just as apparent that after a hint like that, nothing short of dynamite could remove Rhonda from earshot.

"What a lovely idea, Jax," she responded sweetly. "Do come in." She seized his arm in a hold that she intended to look like Anabel's clinging touch—though Kara meant for her grip to hurt. She was disappointed, however, when Jax showed no visible reaction; his muscles felt like warm steel under her hand. "See you later, Rhonda," she said, then led the way through the garage to her back door.

As she fumbled for her keys, she noticed Jax surveying his surroundings and looking bemused. "Guests who invite themselves get the casual treatment around here," she pointed out. "So if you object to going in the back way, you can make an appointment next time." *At least you can try*, she thought.

"I've got no problem with back doors. It's only that I've never before seen a garage neat enough to do brain surgery in. I bet you polish both of your screwdrivers at least once a week, don't you?"

His tone was admiring, but Kara didn't miss the ironic implications. "Keep it up and you'll get to try eating off the floor," she muttered. She snapped on the kitchen lights, washed her hands and started to fill the coffeemaker. "I thought I was supposed to be the one who was desperate to continue our conversation."

"Me, too," Jax said easily. "That's why I was surprised when you disappeared."

"And I'm surprised you noticed."

"I'm a fast learner. I intend to watch my back every minute from now on because, heaven help me, next time you might be armed with a set of nail clippers."

"Cute," Kara said. "I'd have stopped to say thanks, but I figured you had other matters on your mind."

"Anabel, you mean."

"She was a little hard to miss, yes. How'd you find me anyway?"

"You gave Curtis a business card once."

He seemed to have settled in at the breakfast bar, arms folded on the counter, watching her. Though the room had been pleasantly cool when they walked in, it seemed to Kara that the temperature had since gone up by twenty degrees at least.

She fussed around the kitchen till the coffeemaker finished cycling. Apparently, Jax was in no hurry to get to the point and the silence didn't appear to bother him—though it was driving Kara crazy.

When she couldn't stand it anymore, she said, "Why did you do it?" She set a cup in front of him. "Rescue me, I mean. If you'd let them lock me up, you'd have been off the hook completely. So you must have had a reason—and somehow I don't think it was a gentlemanly impulse."

"Since you're quite sure I wouldn't recognize a gentlemanly impulse if it bit me," he said lazily.

Kara winced. "That's not exactly what I meant."

Jax cradled his cup in one big hand. "If you gave it a moment's thought, Kara Jo, you'd realize that I don't want to announce in public that for a couple of minutes I was in mortal fear of a flashlight."

Kara hadn't expected that he'd done it to protect *her*—but the idea that he'd acted simply to protect his image rubbed her like sandpaper. She didn't bother to keep the sarcasm out of her voice. "And here I was hoping against hope that maybe—despite what you said about always wanting something to show for your investment—you were trying to impress me.''

''That hadn't occurred to me, no. It might have eventually, though,'' Jax said genially, ''if I hadn't been too busy considering the advantages of being able to blackmail you.''

Kara almost dropped her cup. ''For what?''

''I could still tell that nice officer all the details. It wouldn't be difficult to convince him that I was too embarrassed to admit in public that I—''

''That's not what I meant. I was asking what I have that you'd want in return for your silence.'' Just a fraction too late, Kara heard the obvious answer echo in her brain and hurried on before he could so much as give her a suggestive smile. ''Of course, you still need a wedding planner, and it would be a bit difficult to find someone else who'd take you on right now.''

''Especially if she heard about the breakup,'' Jax agreed.

''Someone who didn't see the reunion would have legitimate doubts about whether you were really going to patch it up. You know, for a minute there when Anabel first grabbed hold of you, she looked like a woman clinging to a life raft.''

And well she might, Kara told herself uncharitably. Now that she stopped to think about it, it was clear that Anabel had had a narrow escape indeed. Now that she knew a little more about Anabel's circumstances, Kara suspected that the beauty queen had reconsidered as soon as she'd had a chance to cool off. And the moment she'd balanced the thought of Jax Montgomery's money against whatever peccadillo she'd discovered him in, Anabel must have realized what a huge mistake she'd made. The kidnapping report must have seemed heaven-sent; it wasn't every day a woman got such a magnificent opportunity to back down from lofty and self-righteous anger without losing face. And no wonder she'd been so impatient and anxious to get rid of the police; Anabel had some serious fence-mending to do.

"But we didn't," Jax said. "Patch it up, that is."

Kara was so lost in figuring out Anabel's motives that she almost didn't hear what he said. She frowned. "I can't be hearing right. Do you mean to tell me that after that groveling apology of hers, you wouldn't even meet her halfway?"

"It wasn't that, exactly. Once she realized that I hadn't been in serious danger after all—"

"I suppose she remembered why she got mad in the beginning?" Kara shook her head in confusion. "I have to admit that makes me even more curious to know what you did. I can understand her getting mad when she walked in on you doing whatever it was that upset her so. I can see her reacting without thinking and then reconsidering after she'd cooled off—especially when she thought your life might be at risk. But for her to go back to being angry as soon as you were safe—"

"Stranger things have happened." Jax sipped his coffee.

Not with people like Anabel, Kara wanted to say. But even with the engagement apparently still on hold, it might not be the smartest move of her life to insult the ex-future Mrs. Montgomery. "What on earth did you do that was so astronomically unforgivable? Did she find out there were going to be hookers at the bachelor party? No—that would make *me* throw a man over, but I can't imagine it being enough for Anabel to give up all your lovely money. Therefore it must have been even worse. But—"

"You honestly can't think of anything worse? You disappoint me, Kara Jo. I expected—considering your creativity with flashlights—that you had a pretty good imagination."

"So did I," Kara said flatly. "But I have to admit my mind boggles."

Jax grinned. "It is a shame to miss out on the bachelor party."

"Have it anyway. What's stopping you? Just because you're not having a wedding... I still can't believe that it's off, you know. The way she grabbed you—"

"It wasn't entirely a matter of apologies and forgiveness." Jax sounded a little defensive. "There was a smattering of control involved."

Kara stared at him for a long moment. "Oh, now we're getting to the heart of the matter. Anabel thought that once she'd forgiven you, you owed her a promise not to repeat—whatever it was. And you don't agree. Is that it?"

"Let's say I'm disinclined to turn control of my entire life over to Anabel."

"Right. Or any other woman, I'll bet. What I wouldn't give to know what you did!"

"Is that a serious offer, Kara Jo?" His voice was low, with a husky catch. "I could think of a thing or two that might tempt me to tell you."

"I was speaking metaphorically."

"I wasn't."

"That," Kara said tartly, "was obvious. And it's just as well I'm not making a deal because I'd probably be disappointed anyway."

"With the story? Maybe. But as for the rest—"

Kara cut in before he could finish. "So the real reason you came is because we're back where we started, right? The wedding's been canceled and you don't want to pick up the tab. And that's where the blackmail comes in—because if I annoy you anymore about paying for dresses and flowers and photos, you'll turn me in for kidnapping.''

Jax shrugged. "You're making a very logical argument, you know—and a practical one, too. If I pay off all these people, what am I getting for my money?''

"Satisfaction.''

"Not very concrete, is it?''

"So I'll talk Rhonda into giving you the special-order bolt of lavender satin, and you can have it made into sheets. I'm sure you'll be able to use *those* to full effect. Is that better?''

"Thanks all the same," he said dryly. "But in fact, as well as being logical and practical, you're wrong. I didn't say the wedding was off. I mean that if I'm stuck with paying for it anyway—''

"You mean you're agreeing to fork over the cash?'' Kara was dumbfounded. "What convinced you? Mrs. Gleason's cream puffs?''

"It is my humble opinion that this afternoon Mrs. Gleason earned herself an entire year's worth of delicacies from her favorite gourmet market.''

"That's very sweet of you, Jax. I'll give you the address.''

"I meant, of course, considering that it was your neck she saved, that it should be *your* treat.''

Kara started to laugh. "Now I understand why you're a gazillionaire. It's because you insist on getting two cents' value for every penny you spend.''

"Not necessarily double," he mused. "But it's true that when I spend money, I want something to show for it. If I'm stuck paying for a wedding, as seems to be the case, I may as well get some benefit.''

"So we'll throw the reception anyway. The invitations are already out, so you can entertain all your friends at a non-wedding party—"

"That's fine as far as it goes. But it begs the question of the dress, for one."

"I already told you what to do with the dress. Keep it in reserve, and someday—"

"Oh, you're right. Except I'm not thinking in terms of needing it sometime in the distant future. I'm thinking about two weeks from Saturday."

Warning bells started ringing in Kara's brain. "You can't have a wedding without a bride."

"That is a slight problem," Jax admitted. "But only a slight one."

"It doesn't sound so slight to me. If you and Anabel are still at odds—"

"It was your idea," he went on. "You know, going on with the whole thing."

Her head was spinning. "It was *not*."

"You told me only a minute ago that I should have the bachelor party anyway. Now you're talking about holding the reception—"

"That's different from having a full-fledged wedding."

"Not really. Except for one small thing, every piece is already in place."

"*One small thing*? The *bride*? What are you going to do? Advertise? Hold a lottery?"

He shrugged. "You're the expert planner."

Kara swallowed hard. "Are you out of your mind? You want me to find you a wife?"

"Why not?" he said mildly.

Kara stared at him for a full thirty seconds before the pieces clicked together in her brain. She sank onto a tall stool across the breakfast bar from him and started to laugh. "Now I get it. Anabel's holding out for control, convinced that you'll come around in the end. But as soon as there's someone else in the picture, threatening her supposedly secure position, she's the one who will have to compromise—or at least you think she will. You might actually be right, too. The trouble is, you've only got two weeks, and it won't be easy to make Anabel believe that you've fallen for another woman that hard and that fast. *Any* other woman."

"You really think it will be that difficult?" He sounded surprised.

"Come on, Jax. The woman's a beauty queen. She knows very well that women who can compete with her are few and far between."

"There *is* somebody she's already a little sensitive about."

"That would help, I suppose," Kara mused. "Who? An old girlfriend of yours?"

"Not exactly. I meant you."

Kara was speechless.

"Or didn't you notice the glares you were getting this afternoon?"

"Surely you told her what really happened?" Kara saw the answer in his eyes. "You didn't?"

"I thought it might be useful—considering Anabel's state of mind on the other questions at hand—to leave her in some doubt about exactly what we were doing today. I don't think she believes it had much to do with cream puffs."

"She probably thinks it's all part of what she caught you at earlier. I'm not only going to be an unconvicted felon by the time this is over," Kara complained, "but you're not going to leave me a single shred of reputation, either."

"Why would you think I'd want to do that? It would hardly be to my benefit for you to lose your good name. After all, the Schuylers have been the foundation of society in this city for generations. It would be eminently sensible of me to marry Kara Josephine Schuyler."

The name rolled off his tongue with relish, sending shivers down Kara's spine. She said firmly, "You can't expect Anabel to believe that you've suddenly become overwhelmingly attracted to me."

"Not exactly. But she doesn't have to believe that." He sounded quite earnest. "Look at it this way, Kara. Admittedly, you're not Miss World material, but you're not hard on the eyes."

"Gee, thanks."

"We've got a history of sorts. Anabel understands that even if she doesn't know the details. She can see that there's a tension between us—"

"Imagine that," Kara mocked. "What a very perceptive mind she has!"

"And she'll read it as sexual tension." Jax leaned across the breakfast bar and captured a lock of Kara's hair, tugging gently and pulling her closer to him as he slowly wound the hair around his index finger. When she was so close that his lips were almost brushing hers and Kara could scarcely get her breath, he let go and said easily, "See what I mean? Most important of all, you've got a connection with society that—"

"That you don't care a fig for."

"Anabel doesn't know how I feel. And though she wouldn't admit it even under torture, she's envious of your standing. White gloves and all."

"What more could you ask for?" Kara returned dryly. "I'm the perfect woman for you, after all. At least for the moment."

He grinned, teeth gleaming white. His eyes, she saw, held a satisfied sparkle. "Exactly the conclusion I came to, my dear. So how about it? Shall we arrange a little bridal swap?"

CHAPTER FOUR

A bridal swap.

bridal swap?"

CHAPTER FOUR

A BRIDAL swap.

Kara was having trouble getting a full breath, but Jax
sounded as casual about the whole proposition as if he
were merely switching cars. Though, Kara thought, if his
favorite Jaguar *was* at stake, he'd probably take the transaction a great deal more seriously.

Of course, even she had to admit there was good reason
for his offhand attitude. It would be a different thing altogether if he actually intended to go through with this
farce. But since he didn't, why should he get obsessive
about something that was merely the means to an end?

Maybe she shouldn't be taking it so seriously, either,
Kara told herself. It wasn't as if her whole life was at
stake, after all. How long could it possibly take to make
his point to Anabel? A few days? Certainly no longer than
a week. The woman had proved today that, though she
might have a temper, she wasn't exactly slow on the uptake.

Kara felt herself wavering and she frantically tried to
gather her wits. She *couldn't* actually be considering this
mad proposal—could she? She'd be absolutely insane to
go along with it. Just because Jax had missed a great
career opportunity as a mesmerist, enthralling people and
persuading them to do exactly what he wanted no matter
what the cost, Kara wasn't excused from exercising her
common sense—and her common sense told her to run.

On the other hand, a small voice at the back of her
mind advised, this was the simplest answer yet to a very

thorny predicament—one that Kara had begun to think insoluble. Just because in the past couple of hours her own troubles had taken center stage, it didn't mean that the problems that had originally landed her in this difficult situation had gone away. They'd only been pushed aside, and now she found herself facing them squarely again.

The Montgomery-Randall wedding was still off, and unless something changed, it was going to remain that way. Mrs. Gleason, Rhonda, even baby Dylan—to say nothing of all the other people who stood to lose money— were still threatened.

If Kara could prevent the wedding from imploding and wounding all those people—people she had gotten involved in the first place, people to whom she owed her best effort—she had a responsibility to do it.

Up to a certain point, of course. That went without saying. Actually marrying Jax Montgomery would be far beyond the call of duty; in fact, Kara got cold shivers at the very idea. But that wasn't the question. If, by merely pretending to be engaged to him for a few days, she could salvage the situation, wasn't it her obligation to do so?

She studied him as he sat at her breakfast bar drinking his coffee, looking as unconcerned as if they'd been discussing whether it might rain. She said, with only a slight edge to her voice, "How can I possibly think of turning you down?"

"You can't." Jax sounded quite pleased with himself. "Or perhaps I should say that if you can, you've discovered a loophole I missed."

"How flattering it is that you're so determined to pursue this relationship that you've closed off every escape hatch." She reached for the coffeepot to refill his cup, then realized that his eyes had gone dark and unreadable.

"Some women wouldn't be trying to escape, Kara Jo."
His voice held a husky undertone.

Kara's heart gave a strange little flutter. She swallowed
hard and reminded herself that no matter what he said, it
was no excuse for letting herself go all soft and steamy
inside. With that bedroom voice of his, if Jax
Montgomery read aloud the fine print on a breakfast cereal box, he could make it sound seductive.

"Some women like all kinds of weird things," she said
tartly. "Personally, I've never seen the appeal of bond-
age."

Jax picked up his coffee cup and looked at her lazily
over the rim. "Maybe you've never encountered the right
set of handcuffs."

Every muscle in Kara's body tightened into knots.
What have I got myself into now? she wondered frantically, and tried to fight off the mental pictures his words
had created—images of herself helpless, completely in
Jax's power, not struggling against his strength…

Wait a minute, she thought. *Not* struggling? Where had
that notion come from? She'd be scratching and kicking
and screaming…wouldn't she?

His tone was suddenly brisk. "Figuratively speaking,
of course. After this afternoon, I expect you might not
find the real thing very romantic."

"How infinitely considerate of you." Despite her best
efforts, her voice cracked. "What should I expect instead?
Silk ropes?"

His eyebrows rose. "So you do have an imagination
after all. Just don't let it run away with you, darling. I've
never found it necessary to physically restrain my feminine companions and I don't plan to start any time soon.
On the other hand," he added thoughtfully, "if you're

really intrigued by things like silk ropes, I'm sure you could persuade me to give them a try."

Relief left a sudden emptiness in Kara's stomach. "Don't hold your breath. That'll happen about the same time Anabel asks me for beauty tips."

Jax's gaze roamed her face. His eyes grew even darker when he concentrated, Kara realized, and right now they were almost black. If she had an eyebrow hair in need of plucking, Jax wasn't going to miss it.

The inspection annoyed her. It wasn't as if he needed to make a point by comparing her every feature with Anabel's; Kara not only knew perfectly well how far she fell short of the beauty queen's standards, she'd just admitted it to him. So there was no call for him to rub it in by inspecting every eyelash, every skin cell, every pore.

She forced herself to sit still under his scrutiny, but it took the last ounce of willpower she possessed, and she was relieved when he blinked as if coming out of a trance and said briskly, "Now that we have everything settled, let's go out for dinner."

"Actually, I was longing to sink into a warm bath with a good book till I recover. Staying there through the weekend ought to—"

"That's no way to impress Anabel. Unless, of course, you skip the book and invite not only me but the tabloid press to join you."

"It wouldn't be my first choice. Don't you have to go to work or something?" she asked hopefully. "You've had practically the whole day off."

"I don't work all the time."

So much for Rhonda's theories. "More's the pity," Kara muttered. "You know, before we go any further with this, I'd like to make sure we have all the details clear. The instant Anabel comes around and agrees to your terms, I go back to being the wedding planner—right?''

''Not a moment longer.'' Jax's voice was solemn, but he had a twinkle in his eyes that made Kara want to punch him. Did he think she was an idiot, expecting—maybe even hoping—that he might want to extend this mockery of an engagement a millisecond longer than necessary?

''You do realize why I'm asking, don't you?'' she said irritably. ''It's because staying on to finish the job will be a feat in itself. Anabel's not going to be pleased with me and the role I'm playing in this mess, and she'll probably want to fire me.''

''Now that you mention it, I wouldn't be a bit surprised.''

''If she does it, I'm certain to look unreliable and unprofessional because I haven't completed my contract, and incompetent because I was let go. That's a sacrifice I'm not about to make.''

His eyebrows rose slightly.

''So before you start making noises about who's setting the rules here, Jax, let's get this much straight. You're playing this game to make your point with Anabel, which is fine with me. But I'm doing it to save my reputation and my business—not ruin them. So you'll simply have to convince Anabel that whether she likes it or not, I'm in for the duration.''

Jax frowned. ''You do like to issue challenges, don't you?''

''Consider it the acid test to see who'll be the one in charge after you're married,'' Kara recommended. ''No matter what she says she'll do, the truth is that if you give in on this one, you'll be henpecked the rest of your life. So you better make sure you figure out a way to handle it because I intend to carry this wedding through to the end.''

"I couldn't ask for more dedication," he murmured.

"And in the meantime, you aren't going to give me any more grief about paying the bills.''

"I'm not?'' He sounded almost meek.

Kara wasn't fooled. "Stop and think about it, Jax.'' Her voice was firm. "Since you do intend to get married after all, it's greatly to your advantage to keep things in place rather than cancel the entire wedding and start over again later. It's not the financial cost of canceling, it's the inconvenience. So whenever the money's due, I expect that you'll come across with it.''

"There's a certain amount of truth to that," Jax conceded. "Just as long as you don't expect me to pay it all up front—because once I made that mistake, you could thumb your nose at me and do whatever you please.''

"I was afraid you'd think of that.''

He grinned. "So now that we've agreed to distrust each other, what about dinner?''

Kara sighed and slid off the high stool. "I suppose the sooner Anabel hears about this stunt, the sooner I'm off the hook and I can go back to doing my real job.'' She started for the door.

"I'm so glad you're looking forward to it. Where are you going?''

"To change my clothes. Unless you want me to go in rags?''

His gaze drifted over the plain navy blue dress. "You're right. Something a little more up-to-date than that outfit might be a good idea—and something that doesn't call for prim little white gloves.''

"When I said *rags* I meant my hose, not the dress.''

Jax shrugged and reached for the coffeepot. "I assume

you have something a little splashier tucked away somewhere.''

"How splashy do you have in mind? Where are we
going?''

"The Century Club, of course. And don't look at me
that way, I have a jacket and tie in the car.''

"I wasn't worried about your wardrobe. Isn't the
Century Club just a little public?''

The corner of Jax's mouth quirked as he mimicked,
"Isn't *public* the whole point?''

"I mean, this isn't even a dress rehearsal. It's a first
walk-through. I think it would be a wiser to start out a
little more slowly, get our stories straight—''

"Well, if you'd like something more private and personal so we can get better acquainted—like the bathtub—
perhaps...''

The husky suggestion was so seductive that Kara
thought she could smell the perfumed bubbles. "You
never quit, do you, Montgomery? Maybe it's a good thing
Anabel got the shock of her life today. It'll help prepare
her to share you with every female who crosses your line
of sight in the next forty years.''

He came across the room toward her. "Don't sell yourself short, Kara Jo. You're hardly just any—''

She shook her head and held up both hands to fend
him off. "Don't waste your time trying to convince me
I'm not one of the crowd—and a pretty sizable crowd at
that.''

"But you aren't, darling. For one thing, you're the only
woman I'm engaged to at the moment.''

The sheer brazenness of the statement left her reeling.

Jax came closer. "And since the wedding is only a
couple of weeks away, nobody could be offended if

we..." His voice had dropped to a whisper so soft it barely tickled her ear.

Kara tilted her head away and managed to say, "You mean, if we, er, sort of anticipated things?"

"My thought precisely." Jax's lips brushed her throat with fire. "So what's the evening's entertainment going to be, sweetheart?"

"Dinner." Her voice trembled a little. "In fact, I had no idea how much I was looking forward to having dinner with you at the Century Club."

"Good," Jax said briskly. "Go change your clothes."

The man's like a lightning storm, Kara thought. *You know ahead of time it's going to strike, but you can't be quite sure where or how—and you absolutely never see the bolt that hits you!*

She was almost to the door when he said thoughtfully, "It's just as well anyway. I wouldn't have liked to explain to my parents that I missed a dinner date with them because I was seduced over a cup of coffee."

"*You* were sed..." Kara's voice trailed off as his words registered. "What do you mean, *parents*?"

"I have the regulation number, if that's what's puzzling you. One father, one mother. And I have a standing date with them on Thursdays. Actually, it's pretty lucky, I think." His smile was sunny, untroubled. "What better way to start out our engagement than by introducing you to my parents?"

The Century Club was crowded, with cars lined up at the main entrance, waiting for the valets to take over. Kara thought the mansion had never looked more forbidding, and the wait scraped at her nerves till she was ready to scream. "This is a really bad idea, Jax," she said finally.

"Are you nervous about meeting my parents?" Jax

sounded astonished. "I thought the whole point of being a leader of society was that you never met a situation you couldn't handle."

Kara glared at him. "I am not nervous about meeting your parents. I'm anticipating how they're going to feel."

"That's my Kara, always keeping other people's interests at the top of her list. And a very long list it is, too. Mrs. Gleason, the photographer, my parents..."

Kara gritted her teeth. He wasn't being very subtle, but then, he didn't have to be. He might just as well have come straight out and reminded her what would happen if she didn't play by the rules he'd made. She made a last-ditch effort nonetheless. "Look, you've got a cell phone in your pocket, right? Why don't you call the club and have them paged?"

Jax pulled a tie from the glove compartment. "You honestly believe it'll be less of a shock if I give them two minutes' warning before we actually walk in?"

Put that way, it did sound ridiculous. "Only marginally," Kara admitted. "But at least they won't be taken by surprise in the middle of the dining room, with that snooty maître d' and half the membership staring."

"As far as that goes, they'll probably be waiting in the lounge, not the dining room. I must say, though, I'm looking forward to seeing the maître d's face when I appear with you instead of Anabel." Jax patted his tie into place.

"Would you *listen*? How can you be certain your mother won't have a case of hysterics?"

"Because I know my mother. A case of hysterics wouldn't dare attack her."

"A stroke, then. Look, it's bad enough to tell your parents that your engagement's been called off a mere two weeks before the wedding, but to introduce them three seconds later to your fianceé's replacement is worse yet. And to do it all in public—''

''Oh, is that what's upsetting you? That they haven't been warned? It's nice of you to be concerned, but my parents are a couple of tough old birds.''

''What a relief. Knowing that makes me feel *so* much better.'' She realized that sarcasm didn't seem to be making any impression on him, so Kara gave it up.

Jax turned the car over to the valet and came around to open Kara's door.

There's nothing more you can do, she told herself. *If it goes badly, Jax has only himself to blame.*

He took her hand to help her out. ''I must tell you, by the way, that I was completely wrong about the gloves. Of course, when I told you to skip them, I was thinking about the matronly kind—not ones like these.'' His hand skimmed the length of her black silk glove from fingertips to elbow. ''I especially like the peekaboo slit at the wrist.'' He pressed his lips to a small gap between the buttons.

Kara gritted her teeth in an effort not to gratify him by pulling away. But she couldn't control the pulse point in her wrist. ''The slit is only there to make them easier to put on, not turn you on.''

''The truth is you wore them just to annoy me, didn't you?'' Jax murmured.

She saw no point in denying it. ''I suppose I should've expected that no matter what you said about them, gloves would turn you on,'' Kara grumbled. ''After all, everything else seems to.''

He laughed and tucked her hand into the crook of his arm, letting his fingers rest atop hers.

The doorman, she noticed, looked as if he was gulping for air. She wanted to tell him not to believe everything he saw, but Jax swept her past Curtis and into the foyer before she could say a word.

"Why don't you go on in?" she said. "I'll leave my shawl in the cloakroom and join you in a moment."

"Or half an hour? Or whenever you get around to it?"

"Jax, it'll be bad enough discussing this in the clubhouse at all, but as soon as I show up, everybody in sight will be trying to listen in. I thought you might like a minute to talk to your parents privately and explain what's going on."

"And why you're coming to dinner instead of Anabel? I already have."

Kara lost her grip and her silky shawl slithered to the floor. Jax picked it up and solicitously draped it around her shoulders once more.

"I called them while you were getting dressed," he said.

"You could have let me know!"

"But then you wouldn't have had your concern for them to occupy your mind."

"And distract me from thinking about the hoax we're trying to pull off? How thoughtful of you, Jax."

"Surely you didn't really think I'd spring my new fiancée on them right here."

"How should I know what to expect? You said yourself they're tough old birds. Personally, though, I think they must have hides like a rhinoceros to have raised you and survived!"

"You will tell them that, won't you?" Jax sounded delighted. "I'm sure they'll be pleased to know how impressed you were even before you met them."

The lights were dimmer in the lounge than they'd been during the afternoon, but there was no mistaking that the place was almost full and that most of the eyes were on them. Jax paused in the doorway for a moment, looked around, then started across the room to the window overlooking the pool.

To Kara's relief, he didn't stop at the booth she'd been ushered to this afternoon by the policeman. How incredibly long ago all that seemed....

Two tables away, she saw a white-haired man say something to the woman beside him and then stand up as they approached. She hardly noticed the conservative cut of his suit; she was fascinated by his eyes. Jax's eyes, she thought—deep set and dark, but warmer somehow. The woman beside him could never have been conventionally pretty, but she was beautiful. The strong, sharp bones of her face gave her the intriguing look of a modern sculpture.

Tough old birds, Kara thought. She supposed Jax must know what he was talking about, but these two were hardly the image that his description had brought to mind.

Jax drew her forward. "Mother, Dad—this is Kara Schuyler. Kara, Jeannette and John Montgomery."

She'd never been subjected to a gaze quite so intense; Kara found herself giving thanks that this was only make-believe and that everybody at the table knew it. Maybe that was what Jax had meant by calling his parents tough—he certainly ought to know the kind of powerful performance they were capable of.

John Montgomery didn't take his eyes off Kara, but he spoke to his son. "I'd say this is a pleasant surprise, Jackson—except with the wild stories your mother and I have been hearing ever since we got here, I don't think anything would surprise me."

"I'm glad to know you haven't been bored while you waited." Jax bent to kiss his mother's cheek, then seated Kara across the table from Jeannette and fussed with her shawl, draping it carefully over the back of the chair and letting his fingertips trail slowly across her bare shoulders as he settled himself beside her. "So which wild stories have you heard?"

"I couldn't possibly do justice to them." Jeannette Montgomery's voice was low and rich, every bit as sultry in its own way as Jax's.

"Well, it's safe to say that a third of them are probably true," Jax said. "The challenge is always figuring out which third."

"Kara," Jeannette murmured. "It's a pretty name. I was taken aback when Jax called this afternoon and I didn't catch the name then. But I know I've heard it before. I'm sure he's mentioned you."

"Probably not, but Anabel might have. I'm the wedding planner she hired." *Under other circumstances*, Kara thought, *this would be one of the ten most embarrassing moments in my life.*

"And Kara's so good at her job that she can handle any eventuality," Jax added. "So today when I came up short a bride, Kara stepped in to fill the vacancy." The cocktail waitress appeared at his elbow, and he turned to Kara. "I have no idea what you'd like, my dear."

Kara asked for a glass of white wine and thought it was probably lucky she didn't already have one in her hand; she'd have been sorely tempted to pour it over his head. Surely he didn't need to push the envelope quite so far.

"That's it, of course," Jeannette said. "I really had no idea you two had gotten to know each other so well."

"Oh, we haven't," Jax said lightly. "In fact, we just met today—for the first time in over ten years. That's why I don't know what she drinks. I haven't even found out yet whether she prefers tea first thing in the morning or coffee—"

"And I'm not likely to tell you any time soon," Kara said under her breath. "Heaven knows what you could do with that information."

"I didn't ask you to tell me," Jax pointed out. "I'm quite willing to do my research."

By spending the night with you and waking up in your arms... He didn't have to actually say it; the meaning was as clear as a summer's day.

She shouldn't have been surprised, Kara told herself, that in the midst of a crowd of curious onlookers—and within three feet of his parents, for heaven's sake!—the man was trying to seduce her. It was as natural to him as breathing.

At least he'd been gentleman enough to imply that they *weren't* sleeping together...yet. Though, considering he'd also made it clear there simply hadn't been enough time, she wasn't sure she owed him any thanks.

"You just met this morning?" Jeannette was looking a little glassy-eyed.

Kara was certain it had nothing to do with the cocktail sitting before Jeannette almost untouched; she was uncomfortably familiar with the feeling herself.

"On the driving range. It was like..." Jax was obviously groping for a comparison.

Kara, terrified he'd come up with something to do with guns or hostage holding, heard herself say, "Like being struck by lightning."

The brilliance in Jax's eyes was almost blinding. Kara suspected it was caused by suppressed laughter. "Was it like that for you, too?" he murmured. "And here I thought I had to win you over with my charm!"

"I think," John Montgomery said firmly, "that it's time for dinner." He pushed back his chair, cast a thoughtful glance around the room and offered his arm to Kara. "Welcome to the family, my dear."

The twinkle in his eyes warmed Kara's heart. *Thank heaven*, she thought, *nobody's taking this seriously. Maybe, even after this farce is over, we can actually be friends.*

She told herself that the hollowness inside her was only a remnant of her fear and would go away very soon.

The maître d's expression was everything Jax could have wished for; as he showed them to their table, the man looked as if he had a lemon wedge caught in his throat. His reaction was understandable, though. If—as Jax suspected—Kara had made a habit of dressing like a middle-aged matron whenever she met with Anabel, it was no wonder if the sight of her in a halter-topped bright pink dinner dress had made the maître d' choke up.

Jax leaned back in his chair and looked directly across the table at Kara. She no doubt thought she'd maneuvered herself into that seat—avoiding his company even at the cost of surrounding herself with his parents. That was all right, he decided. He wouldn't bother to tell her that if she hadn't sought out that seat, he'd have arranged it for her.

Not that he wouldn't have enjoyed sitting beside her and watching the delicate play of color in her face as he teased her. But there was something to be said for taking it easy, too. With Kara occupying a hundred percent of his parents' attention, he was free to let his gaze roam.

At least half the people in the dining room were sneaking looks at the Montgomerys' table, he noted. Among them he saw several of Anabel's crowd—one with an unattractively open mouth. So the word would get back to her in record time. That ought to please Kara....

He glanced over at her to see if she'd noticed, but she was talking animatedly to his mother. "...Weddings and the associated celebrations," she was saying. "Recently, I've been doing more charity fund-raisers. I don't make any money from them, though. I won't charge a fee because that would take resources from a good cause."

"But doing things like that must be a wonderful boost for the reputation."

Kara nodded. "And they always end up leading to new business, so I guess I can't pretend to be completely virtuous about volunteering my time."

"But if you prefer doing weddings..." Jeannette began thoughtfully.

"The trouble with weddings is they're pretty much one to a customer—the elaborate ones anyway, involving the kind of display that people hire me to produce. So I'm always looking for leads to new business. That's why I do sweet-sixteen parties."

"Because girls who turn sixteen will be getting married a few years down the road," Jeannette agreed.

"That's very farsighted of you," John said. "Looking a decade ahead."

He sounded, Jax thought, as if he'd like to applaud.

Kara smiled. "I intend to be doing this at least that long."

"But surely..." Jeannette's brow furrowed; then she seemed to think better of it. "While we're talking of parties, Kara, the kind I put on are nothing compared with yours, I'm sure. But we're having a barbecue on Saturday afternoon. You'll come, won't you?"

"Saturday?" Kara shook her head. "I'm sorry, but I have an appointment that afternoon." She glanced across the table at Jax. "I think I mentioned Donald Sloan to you?"

It was John who answered. "The one who builds the precision razors, you mean?"

Kara nodded. "I'm planning to talk to him and his wife about a sweet sixteen party for their daughter. That one could lead not only to a wedding someday but to all kinds of work for her father's corporation. So I'm afraid I couldn't—"

"A talk with Donald Sloan won't take all day," Jax said.

"Look, Jax, I already know you think it's a waste of time to try for his business, but—"

"I only meant that the barbecue's guaranteed to be going on no matter what time your appointment's finished. I'll take you out to Sloan's before the party. You can impress him by showing up with a chauffeur."

"Please come," Jeannette said. "All the family will be there."

Kara looked confused. "The family?"

"And they'll be very anxious to meet you," Jeannette went on comfortably. "You can let me know then what I can do to help."

"Help?" Kara's voice was cool.

Danger signs flashed in Jax's brain, but it was too late.

"Yes. Canceling the wedding and starting over will be a big job, even for a professional. Of course, all the new arrangements won't have to be made at once, but I'm sure some help will come in handy nonetheless. I don't suppose—since you haven't even gotten a ring yet—that you've discussed a wedding date?"

Kara, he noted, wasn't even looking at his mother. She was staring straight at him, and her expression made him wonder if he'd suddenly sprouted fangs. He didn't need to be psychic to know what she was thinking, either. *You didn't tell her this is all a stunt to get Anabel back, did you?*

Oops, he thought. Let a man overlook one little thing, and just watch what happened to him.

"As a matter of fact," he said, "we have. Two weeks from Saturday. We're not canceling anything."

"That's absurd, Jackson," Jeannette said firmly. "Weddings are a very personal affair, and I'm sure with all her experience Kara has some pretty definite ideas about what she'd like."

"What's absurd about it? Kara's arranged the whole affair—and she was telling me only a couple of hours ago how it was far more sensible to follow the original plans than to start all over. Weren't you, darling?"

Kara's eyes had gone turbulent, as if tranquil ocean waters had been suddenly hit by a hurricane. But she said gamely, "Rescheduling everything would be a nightmare. It'll be so much simpler just to go ahead..."

She's a trouper, Jax told himself happily. Of course, he'd known that all along.

Nevertheless, he predicted, it should be a very interesting couple of weeks.

CHAPTER FIVE

IT WAS only by biting her tongue till it ached that Kara was able to stay silent until the Jaguar was rolling down the Century Club's driveway and the elder Montgomerys were no more than a blur in the mirror.

"You didn't tell your parents this supposed engagement of ours is a hoax," she accused. Fury made her voice tremble.

"Of course not." Jax sounded no more than mildly interested. "They're much more convincing in the role because they really believe it."

"That's cruel, Jax! To put them through this—"

"I'm not only old enough to make my own decisions, Kara, but my parents have respected that fact for a number of years now." His voice was dry.

"Since you made your first million, I suppose. Well, I don't doubt they believe in the general philosophy of not interfering in a grown son's life. But actually watching someone you care about make a fool of himself is a different thing altogether."

"On the basis of one evening together, you know them very well. Or at least you think you do."

The faint irony in his tone made Kara color with annoyance.

"My experience with them," Jax said, "suggests that they'll reserve judgment. Besides, it's only for a little while."

"And I'm sure it will be a great deal of comfort when you tell them I'm out and Anabel's back in. You know, you're going to get a reputation for being fickle, Montgomery, switching fiancées as often—*oftener*—than you change your socks.''

"As long as I restrict myself to one at a time..."

Kara was hardly listening. "And I played straight into your hands. I could just kick myself for making the whole thing a great deal worse."

"You're feeling guilty? What for?"

"For letting them believe it was real, of course. I thought your parents were simply wonderful actors, just following the script. So I did the same. I acted like a fool—"

"By doing what? Being yourself? Honestly, Kara, what would you have done differently if you'd known they think we're really engaged? I'll tell you. You'd have been all starchy and proper and watchful, and nobody looking on would've believed a stitch of it."

She was momentarily chastened. That was, after all, the whole point, wasn't it? To convince the outsiders, who would then report back to Anabel?

But arranging a public scenario to convince Anabel was one thing, while exploiting his parents—that was something else.

Still, Kara reminded herself, Jax's conduct wasn't any of her business. Nothing about the Montgomery family was. But her own feelings were a different matter. She had a right to be angry at the way he'd manipulated her.

"I don't appreciate your making me lie to your mother like that."

"You weren't lying," Jax pointed out. "You didn't know all the facts, so how could you lie about what was going on? Besides, even if you were lying, I don't see why it should bother you."

Kara was shocked speechless, and it took a moment for

her to hear the question he'd really been asking. Why *was* it so monumentally important that she be absolutely straightforward with a woman she'd see, at most, a half-dozen times in the next couple of weeks? A woman she would likely never again encounter once the wedding was done with?

"You know, I have absolutely no idea why I don't like deceiving people," she said tartly. "I guess it's just become a habit to tell the truth. Tell me, how did you get rid of your conscience so completely, Jax? You obviously have—because it certainly gave *you* no qualms to lie to her, did it?"

"My mother learned long ago not to jump to conclusions."

"A matter of self-preservation, no doubt," Kara said dryly.

"And this is all in a good cause anyway."

Kara turned that one over in her mind and ended up more confused than ever. "Does that mean your mother likes Anabel so much that you don't want to upset her with the details of your little scheme, or that she doesn't like her at all?"

"Does it matter?"

"Probably not. I'm sure it won't influence your plans in the least." Irritably, Kara shifted in her seat and tried another tack. "Doesn't it bother you that your mother's so plainly unhappy about what you're doing?"

"Not when it's wedding plans she's unhappy about. What's wrong with the arrangements anyway? Anabel certainly paid for the best."

"And she's getting it," Kara said, automatically defensive. "There's nothing wrong with the things she wanted. But your mother's right. Tastes in weddings are completely individual. There is no one-size-fits-all when it comes to walking down the aisle. If there's even an aisle—that's only one of the variables.''

"So educate me. What would you do differently?"

"If it was really my wedding?" Kara sighed. "I'd cut out ninety percent of the trimmings and make it very, very simple.''

He turned to stare at her. "You're kidding."

"Would you mind watching the road, Jax? And why do you think I'm joking?"

"Because it's your job to talk brides into these elaborate productions. You can't expect me to believe you don't want one yourself.''

"I don't talk anybody into anything, Jax. I explore what the bride wants and help her have the day of her dreams while staying within her budget.''

"I'd think you'd be afraid of putting yourself out of business.''

"Not a chance. Even a very simple ceremony takes a good deal of planning—and the fact is, most brides aren't interested in *simple*. They want to put on the biggest show they can afford.''

"But not you."

"You want the truth, Jax? I've seen so many exotic displays, I'm getting pretty cynical about them. The less pageantry there is, the fewer things can go wrong, so—''

"You'd leave out the dozen bridesmaids?"

"Thirteen—Anabel added another one last week. Didn't she tell you you'd need another usher? If I was superstitious," Kara mused, "I'd wonder if that was where things started going wrong. And I'd settle for one kind of cake instead of six—''

"I didn't know there *were* six kinds of wedding cake."

"Butter cream, chocolate, spice, raspberry torte, coffee, and peppermint twist.'' She ticked them off on her fingers. "If the baker had offered eighteen, Anabel would have had all the others, as well. Instead of swarms of guests and a country-club dance, I'd have the few most important people in my life and a string quartet—"

"It sounds like an entirely different wedding," Jax admitted.

"That's precisely the point your mother was making."

"But you see, that's why I don't understand. I've heard Mom say a dozen times that it isn't the wedding that's important, it's the marriage. So what difference does it make whether it's simple or elaborate? A wedding's a wedding. Isn't it?"

And this one's beginning to look like a comic opera, she thought. *Complete with interchangeable brides...*

Kara surrendered. Why waste time trying to make him understand? Even if she got through to him, nothing was going to change. This was still Anabel's wedding, after all. If she wasn't just being a temporary replacement for Anabel, it would be different, of course, but—

Darn right it would be different, Kara told herself. *For one thing, I wouldn't be arguing with him about the ideology of weddings. I'd be using all my breath for a getaway!*

"Not that any of this discussion actually matters," she said. "As it stands, you've not only stuck me with the production of the century, you've arranged it so I have to look positively happy about it, too."

He looked thoughtful. "Would it help if I said I want you to honestly like your ring?"

"You mean you're not going to call up Anabel and ask for hers back? She's supposed to return it, you know, since she's the one who broke the engagement."

"I could, I suppose, if you'd really like to wear it instead of a new one."

Kara pressed her fingertips to her temples. "I was joking, Jax. She'd smash it before she'd hand it over for me to wear, and that's hardly the result you have in mind, is it? Anyway, what does it matter whether I like the ring? It's only window dressing."

"I'll take you to the jewelers tomorrow."

"Why? Don't you trust me to stay inside a budget? Not that the cost will be important."

A tiny frown tugged at his eyebrows. "What makes you say that?"

"Well, it's not the fact that you're a gazillionaire, that's for sure. I just meant that you'll be able to take the ring back in a week or so—probably before the bill even arrives."

"I hadn't considered that little advantage."

"You mean I actually beat you to a penny-saving measure?"

He smiled. "Take your bow, Kara. Is noon all right? We'll have lunch before we do our shopping."

"At Anabel's favorite restaurant, of course."

"How'd you guess? I so wanted to surprise you."

"I thought you worked," Kara grumbled. "And I certainly do, so—"

"Work?" Jax said as if he didn't recognize the word. "Damn, you're right. I not only have to show up at the office tomorrow, I also have a meeting that's likely to drag on into the night. How about Saturday before the barbecue? I'll pick you up."

Kara didn't answer directly. "That's another thing," she said. "The barbecue. The very idea of being paraded around in front of your whole family as your intended bride, when you know perfectly well that by next week it'll all be different…"

Jax parked the Jaguar in front of her duplex and came

around to open her door. "You don't have to manufacture problems for us to talk about," he said mildly. "I'll happily come in, Kara, and stay as long as you like. All you have to do is ask. Now what were you saying about the barbecue?"

Kara glared at him. "I just can't wait for Saturday," she said sweetly. "In fact, I'll be so busy dreaming about the barbecue that I won't have a single thought to spare for you—so there's certainly no point in your coming in. Good night, Jax."

His soft laugh followed her up the sidewalk to her front door.

She'd forgotten to leave a light on, and only the faint glow of a streetlamp helped as she fumbled in her tiny evening bag for her key. She could imagine what Jax would say if she had to admit she'd locked herself out. He'd probably think she'd done it on purpose.

She would look like a fool, standing on the step with her penlight in hand, surveying the contents of her bag. Except she'd forgotten the flashlight, too; her groping fingers found only tissues, her tiny makeup case and—finally—the hard outline of her key. She slipped it into the lock and as the door opened she tried to ignore Jax's quiet parting words from the street.

"Good night, darling. If you get tired of dreaming about the barbecue, call me. I'll rush right over to be a substitute."

She slammed the door and sank against it.

Just this morning, she reflected ruefully, life had looked so simple.

Rhonda arrived with two cinnamon rolls in a basket, the baby in a sling on her chest and Kara's morning newspaper under her arm. "It's barely the crack of dawn,"

Kara protested as she answered the door. "What are you doing up at this hour?"

"That's a very good question," Rhonda said cheerfully. "Bear with me while I answer it. Dylan decided to walk the floor all night—which requires a bit of cooperation from Mom or Dad since he's a long way from being able to walk by himself. And since Jeff has an exam today, I was the lucky one who got to pace from the living-room window to the back door, patting the baby's back and getting an eyeful of everything that was going on in the vicinity, including my next-door neighbor wearing silk gloves and getting out of a dark blue Jaguar—"

"So you know that Jax Montgomery didn't stay the night."

"Interesting," Rhonda mused, "how that was the first thing that came to your mind. So you thought about letting him stay, did you?"

Kara was nonplussed. "I'm not even awake, Rhonda, so of course my mind isn't tracking right. And no, I didn't consider letting him stay."

"Nevertheless, watching the goings-on left me with a question that interfered with any possibility of sleep. So here I am. Have you put the coffee on yet?"

"No, but I will." Kara led the way to the kitchen. "If you're wondering about the status of the bridesmaids' dresses—"

"Actually, I'd managed to figure that one out by myself," Rhonda said. "It's a serious no-brainer that if you're dating Jax Montgomery, Anabel's not going to need—"

"I'm not. Dating Jax, that is."

"That didn't look like a business conference last night."

"Things aren't always what they look like."

Rhonda rolled her eyes in obvious disbelief. "Whatever you say, dear."

"And if it's the money you're worried about, don't fret. You'll get paid. I didn't have a chance to deal with it yesterday, but as soon as—"

"No, you looked as if you had other things on your mind."

That's not the half of it, Kara wanted to say. "But I'll get a reimbursement check for you as quickly as I can. In the meantime, you may as well finish the dresses."

Rhonda's eyes widened. "Whatever for?"

"Because they're no good to anybody in pieces. I told you, just because you saw me with Jax last night doesn't mean anything's changed."

"Oh, I'm glad you explained *that*," Rhonda murmured. "I might have been confused otherwise. Anyway, surprising as it might be, I didn't come over to ask about either the dresses or the money. If you recall you agreed to baby-sit tonight so Jeff and I could sneak out to a movie. But if you've changed your plans, I'll need to find another sitter—"

"It did slip my mind," Kara admitted. "But I'm not backing out on you. Of course I'll keep Dylan tonight."

"Great. I don't think he'll be any trouble." Rhonda looked down at the snoring baby cradled against her chest and added with a twinkle in her eyes, "He'll no doubt sleep through the evening just so he can entertain me all night again—so you and Jax will practically be alone anyway."

Kara had just settled into the rocker in the bay window at the front of her living room to give Dylan his evening bottle when the doorbell rang. She gave the curtains a twitch and, seeing who was standing on the step, growled a little and shifted the protesting baby onto her shoulder so she could open the door.

"Do the words 'Please phone before dropping in' mean anything to you?" she asked.

Jax smiled down at her. "A mere formality. After all, we *are* engaged. If I can't drop in on my fiancée…" He stepped across the threshold before she could close the door in his face.

"I thought you said your meeting would last into the night."

"I broke it up early. And a good thing, too—or I wouldn't have discovered what you've been hiding from me." He touched the baby's silky hair. "Where'd you have him stashed yesterday?"

"With his mother next door. Remember?" Kara returned to her rocking chair, cradling the baby. Before she could pick up Dylan's bottle, he began rooting eagerly at her breast. She colored and tried not to look at Jax as she offered Dylan the bottle.

"He seems a trifle confused about who's who," Jax observed.

Trust him not to have missed that little display, Kara thought. "Dylan's confused about almost everything." Her voice was dry. "Of course, he's only six weeks old. What's your excuse?"

"For being confused? On the contrary, my dear. I know exactly what I'm doing. I thought perhaps we could go out for dinner tonight, take in a nightclub, maybe dance—"

"Sorry. I've already got a date for the evening. You'll have to call earlier next time."

"He wouldn't be in the way. Well, maybe a little bit on the dance floor, though I'm sure we could work around it. If women who are nine months pregnant can do a tango…'' He leaned against the mantel. "You called me at the office today but didn't leave a message.''

"I forgot about your meeting or I wouldn't have bothered.''

"So of course I rushed right over as soon as my secretary told me you'd tried to reach me. What did you need?''

"It's a little matter of money.''

Jax shook his head sadly. "And here I thought you were pining for my company.''

"Nope, only your checkbook. I was going to give Anabel a number of bills yesterday, before things got sidetracked.''

"Sidetracked,'' he mused. "Interesting way to put it. What do you want me to pay for now?''

"The list is on my desk.'' She pointed toward the dining room, where a large table served as a work surface. "The main one is money Rhonda had to advance for shipping charges on a bolt of satin.''

"Not the fabric itself?''

"No, that'll be later, when it actually comes.''

"You want me to pay for a chunk of material that hasn't even arrived yet. Why not cancel it instead?''

"And tell Anabel she can't have her thirteenth bridesmaid? Are you just hyperventilating, or have you decided to put your foot down to prove who's boss? Anyway, it's too late—special orders have their own set of rules. And since it's putting pressure on Rhonda to be out of pocket, yes, I expect you to pay it now. It's not her fault Anabel didn't plan far enough ahead to order that bolt with the rest.''

"I suppose next you'll expect me to keep on paying you.''

"I'm still doing the same work,'' Kara pointed out.

He grinned. "Ah, but there's a difference."

"Yes, now that I think of it, there is. I'm doing even more than I would have been otherwise. I'll have to re-figure my bill."

"Don't forget to factor in the perks you're getting."

"What perks?"

"Well, I know you don't have your ring yet, but—"

"You mean you're going to lend it to me rent free?" Kara said in mock astonishment. "What a deal! If you're not planning to pay me, Jax, don't complain if I'm not available because I'm involved in other business, trying to keep my cash flow going."

"Business like Donald Sloan? That reminds me, Kara. What time shall I pick you up tomorrow? It'll take a while to select your ring, maybe get it sized, and then another half hour or so to drive out to the Sloan place. What time is your appointment?"

"Two in the afternoon. But there's no reason you have to go."

"Oh, no—I'm not taking the chance that you'll disappear for a couple of days and then tell me you've been sitting on Donald Sloan's terrace drinking mint juleps."

"Might I be? I thought you said he doesn't entertain."

"He doesn't. So if you say the wrong thing you might end up being held captive in an attic somewhere instead."

"Getting only bread and water?"

"Exactly. The thing is, now that I've found you, I can't possibly take the chance—"

He sounded almost serious, Kara thought. She wouldn't have been surprised if he'd put his hand over his heart and let his voice tremble. "That I'll seize the excuse to skip your mother's barbecue," she finished.

Jax grinned. "You got it."

"Have you been there? To the Sloans' house?"

"Just once, years ago. It's quite the place. It might not impress you, with all your experience, but I'll admit it intimidated the heck out of me."

"You know Donald Sloan, then?"

"Not exactly. I was delivering a new sofa."

"You did that, too?"

"I've done a little bit of everything, my dear. I've met him since, but I don't think anybody really knows him. He's not much for socializing on anyone's turf—he never even shows up at Chamber of Commerce functions. In fact, I'm surprised he's allowing his daughter a sweet-sixteen party, much less getting involved with it himself."

"The appointment is very clearly with both Mr. and Mrs. Sloan. That's why I think it's so important. It has to be about something more than a simple party for a couple of dozen teenagers. Will you help me, Jax?"

"Give you a reference, you mean?"

"Not exactly," Kara said slowly. "I guess I want your advice. How to approach him. What not to say."

"I suggest you skip the details and stick to the big picture. He gets bored easily—a lot of CEOs do."

"But I'll have to talk details. Find out what they want, what they don't like. My whole job is details."

Jax shrugged. "So take me along. If you and Mrs. Sloan get into discussing how many balloons to hang on each chandelier—"

"Please, you don't really mean balloons, surely? She's sixteen years old, not five."

"Whatever. If you get bogged down in detail, Donald and I can slide off into shoptalk."

"You'd do that for me?"

"Don't worry about it," he said lightly. "I'll think of something I want in return."

There was a caressing note in his voice that sent shivers

up Kara's spine. "I'm sure you'd have no trouble with *that*." It was too bad, she thought. For a minute there, she'd actually been looking forward to having his help.

"Starting with ice cream. If I can't talk you into dinner, the least you can do to keep me from starving is let me take you out for a waffle cone."

She glanced at the clock. Rhonda and Jeff wouldn't be home for a while, baby Dylan was so sound asleep in her arms that they could load him onto a rocket to the moon and he wouldn't notice, and ice cream sounded good. "Why not?"

By the time Jax had wrestled the baby's car seat into place in the Jaguar, he was muttering about delivery services and Kara was trying not to giggle. "We could just walk," she suggested. "There's a fast-food place a couple of blocks from here—"

"You call the stuff they serve ice cream?" He emerged triumphant and held her door for her. "I am going to introduce you to the real thing, my dear."

Apparently, she soon realized, he was prepared to drive forever in order to do so. "You know, I did tell Rhonda she could pick the baby up at eleven," she said as they entered the third ring of suburbs. "So if you're planning to drive all the way to California, you'd better give me your cell phone so I can leave a message for her."

"Here we are." He pulled the car up next to the most weather-beaten building Kara had ever seen—a converted gas station that leaned so far it appeared to defy gravity. The parking lot, however, was almost filled with cars. "What would you like—chocolate, vanilla, or a combination of the two?"

"I don't suppose they have the kind with bits of bubble gum in it."

"Bubble gum ice cream?" Jax wrinkled his nose in distaste.

"I thought you'd approve," she murmured. "You know, getting two treats for the price of one."

He came back a few minutes later with two enormous cones and a handful of napkins. "I just remembered there's a jewelry store in the strip mall across the street," he said. "We could save ourselves a lot of time and trouble tomorrow if we can find a ring tonight."

It figured, she thought, that he'd consider an engagement ring nothing more than a nuisance, an item to be checked off his to-do list. Then she caught herself up short. Under the circumstances, what else could it be? It wasn't as if the thing had any *meaning*.

With Dylan in the baby sling on Kara's chest, they window-shopped while they ate their ice cream. A few customers were in the store, but it wasn't crowded; as soon as they went inside, a clerk approached with a smile. "Can I show you something in particular?" She looked knowingly at the baby. "Some of our special items for mothers, perhaps?"

"Nice idea," Jax agreed. "But I think we'd better get the engagement ring first." He zeroed in on a display of sparkling diamonds.

The clerk unlocked the case and reached for a tray of rings. "Anything here that catches your fancy? Diamonds? Colored stones? And are you looking for a matching wedding band?"

"Oh, no," Kara said, "just an engagement ring."

A matron at the next case, fingering a string of pearls, sniffed haughtily. "I'd say it's well past time for engagements," she said under her breath.

"Do you mean because of the baby?" Jax asked her ingenuously. "I'm doing the best I can to persuade her to marry me. But she wants to delay the wedding till the boy's old enough to carry her white satin train up the aisle, so the best I've been able to do is convince her to be engaged in the meantime.''

Kara saw the wicked sparkle in his eyes, but not in time to take evasive action. Before she could move, he'd slid an arm around her shoulders and pulled her close. "Isn't that right, darling?'' he murmured, and kissed her long and thoroughly.

At first, his lips were still cool from his ice cream, and he tasted of chocolate. But neither sensation lasted; within moments, Kara felt herself start to sizzle with the heat that sprang up between them, and suddenly, instead of chocolate, she found herself savoring a taste far more exotic and addictive—and purely Jax.

The matron glared at them both, slammed the string of pearls down on the black velvet display board and walked out of the store.

The clerk who'd been waiting on her looked stunned. "Thanks a lot,'' she told Jax.

"My pleasure,'' he murmured. "She wouldn't have looked good in that necklace anyway. She didn't have the throat for it.'' He released Kara and turned back to the display of rings. "See anything you like?''

She was still staring after the matron. True, the woman had been nosy and judgmental and rude. And if Jax hadn't beaten her to the punch, Kara wouldn't have minded pointing that out herself. But the matron's snippy attitude was hardly the fault of the poor clerk, who'd lost her chance at a sizable commission.

Jax picked up a big emerald, turning it to catch the light.

Kara eyed the tiny tag attached to the shank of the ring, trying to interpret the coded information. "There aren't any prices marked," she said finally. "At least, not that I can read."

Jax sounded only mildly interested. "I thought you said the cost didn't matter."

"It certainly doesn't," the clerk who was putting away the pearls said under her breath, "as long as you're only browsing and driving away other customers for fun."

"Oh, the price isn't important," Kara said airily, "as long as it's more expensive than the ring you gave Anabel. But if I can't see the prices, then the gaudier the better, I suppose." She picked up an enormous sapphire.

Jax took it away from her and put it back into the tray. "I absolutely insist that it at least look real," he said calmly, and reached for a marquise diamond so huge and so stunning that it needed no accenting stones.

"That's the most expensive ring in the store," the clerk said.

She sounded, Kara thought, as if she half expected Jax to make a run for it, ring in hand.

He slipped the gleaming band onto Kara's finger and studied it. "I think it'll do. Unless you hate it?"

How silly, she chided herself, to get a lump in her throat over a careless gesture and a meaningless ring! "It's fine," she managed.

"We'll take this," Jax told the astonished clerk. "And wrap up that string of pearls, as well."

Kara's jaw dropped. She didn't find her voice until they were back in the car and headed toward her duplex. "I don't believe you actually did that," she said. "Bought the pearls, I mean, and gallantly saved the poor clerk the commission you'd cheated her out of."

"Did you think that's what I was doing? Sorry to disappoint you, Kara Jo, but I wasn't rescuing the clerk. I was saving the necklace from a fate worse than death. If you were a nice rope of pearls, how would you like to be hanging around that nasty old woman's stringy neck?''

"Now that you mention it..." In fact, his denial shouldn't have come as a surprise, Kara reflected. Of course he'd bought the necklace because he felt a smidgen guilty. But even torture probably wouldn't make Jax Montgomery acknowledge openly that he'd actually yielded to a gentlemanly impulse.

"Besides," Jax mused, "in a couple of weeks, I'll be needing a nice bride's gift, and you just can't go wrong with pearls.''

And so he'd bought Kara a ring and Anabel a string of pearls, all at the same time. One visit to the store, one sales ticket, one entry on his credit card—culminating in two gifts for two very different women. How like him *that* was.

Sometimes, Kara told herself firmly, his ideas of efficiency could be downright annoying.

The red light on Kara's answering machine was blinking furiously when they came in. She considered ignoring it as she would have if she'd invited a date in for coffee, but on second thought, she crossed the room to play her messages. It hadn't been her idea for Jax to occupy her evening, she reminded herself, and if he hadn't shanghaied her into going out for an ice-cream cone and an engagement ring, she'd have been there to answer the phone. He could defer to her business for a change.

As soon as she heard the gentle quaver of Mrs. Gleason's voice asking her to call as soon as possible, Kara glanced at her wristwatch and sighed. "I wonder if she's been hearing rumors.''

The doorbell rang.

"She sounded as if it was something important," Jax observed.

"She sounded downright worried. But it's too late to call her tonight." Kara opened the door.

From the front step, Rhonda said, "The kid's six weeks old and I'm already waiting up nights for him to get home—this is ridiculous, you know." Kara saw Rhonda's eyes widen, and she glanced over her shoulder to see Jax stretched full length on her sofa with Dylan pillowed on his chest. "Well, that explains a couple of things," Rhonda murmured.

"Like what?" Kara asked warily. Belatedly, she tucked her left hand deep in a pocket and out of sight.

"For one, the Jaguar parked in your driveway."

Kara relaxed a trifle.

"And also the phone call I got a few minutes ago," Rhonda said. "From Anabel—canceling the bridesmaids' dresses. So, Kara my dear, are you still expecting me to believe that nothing's changed around here?"

CHAPTER SIX

KARA felt as if the floor had caved in under her feet. She clutched the doorknob like a life preserver as emotions washed over her. First came relief; this was a message Jax couldn't fail to understand. If Anabel had once and for all made up her mind not to marry him, then the reason for this elaborate masquerade was gone, and the whole thing could be over with by midnight.

Of course, reminded a small and relentless voice in the back of her brain, in that case she'd be squarely where she'd started, with a canceled wedding and a groom who was less than thrilled about footing the bills. Relief gave way to annoyance. Everything had been under control until Anabel had poked her nose in once more. What business was it of hers?

Belatedly, Kara listened to herself and started to smile at the absurdity of it all. *Just because it used to be her wedding, the woman seems to think she has a right to an opinion*!

To tell the truth, though, the fact that Anabel was concerning herself at all left her thoroughly confused. "She told me she didn't want anything else to do with it," Kara mused. "So why did she sudddenly decide to dabble in the mess again?"

"*It* and *the mess* both refer to the wedding, I assume?" Rhonda asked. "Not that it comes as any real surprise that it's off."

Kara wasn't listening. "Why would she bother?"

Jax hadn't moved from his relaxed position on the sofa.

101

"I did warn you that Anabel has a tendency to want to control things and people."

"Oh, you think she's heard, so that's why she's doing this?"

"Heard what?" Rhonda asked.

"Remember the redhead who was at the next table last night?"

Kara frowned. "Not especially."

"You had other things on your mind," Jax conceded. "That was one of Anabel's best friends. Of course she's heard."

"Heard what?" Rhonda repeated. Her voice had gotten louder.

"That far from being canceled, the Montgomery wedding is taking place precisely as planned." Jax shifted the baby's weight and stood up to flourish a bow in Kara's direction. "Well, with one small change. The curtain will go up as scheduled, but the part of the bride will be played by Miss Randall's understudy, Ms. Kara Schuyler."

Rhonda stared at him, wide-eyed, for a full thirty seconds. Finally, under her breath, she said, "And I actually left my baby with you two lunatics? May heaven forgive me." She scooped up Dylan's diaper bag, took the infant from Jax's arms and without another word let herself out of the duplex.

Silence fell over the living room. Jax sat down on one end of the sofa and Kara sank onto the other.

"You'd think, from her reaction, that there was something really strange about this," Jax commented.

Kara ignored him. "I wonder what else Anabel's canceled."

"Mrs. Gleason for one. I suppose that's why her message sounded perturbed."

"Of course that's why. I'm just surprised everybody

else hasn't called, too. Does that mean Anabel's only getting started? Or that she only called Rhonda and Mrs. Gleason?''

"Maybe when the machine answered, the others thought you were out of town and simply hung up.''

"Oh, now there's a comforting thought." In her mind, Kara ran down the list of all the suppliers she'd have to call tomorrow morning. It wasn't going to be fun to feel her way through each conversation, because in case Anabel *hadn't* issued cancellation orders to everyone, Kara would only create trouble for herself by bringing up the possibility.

"You know, Jax,'' she said, "maybe you should call her bluff. Since she's already let the cat out of the bag, why not end this entire charade and see what she does next? I'm betting it'll bring her around in a hurry—and it would be so much easier than carrying on this performance."

He appeared to think it over. "You might be right."

Kara's jaw dropped. *I absolutely cannot be hearing properly*, she thought. "You mean you agree? It was that easy?''

"I agree it would probably be simpler to call everything off. I didn't say that's what we were going to do.''

"I should have known,'' Kara grumbled.

"Because nothing's really changed since yesterday. All the same arguments apply—plus a new one.''

"Let me guess. You've decided this attack of Anabel's is really only a diversionary tactic, and it means that she's changed her mind and is coming around.''

"I hadn't considered that possibility exactly. I was thinking about the fact that I just invested ten thousand dollars in a bride's gift, which will be totally useless unless there's a wedding.''

"Give the damned necklace to your mother for her birthday," Kara said a little wildly. "*Her* throat is still in great shape to show off pearls. And if you're worried about this spotlight of a ring I'm wearing, I'll happily take it back tomorrow morning."

Jax shook his head sadly. "Where would that get me? After all this effort and plotting and scheming, I'd still be in exactly the same position I was yesterday when you stuck the flashlight in my back."

Precisely what she'd already told herself—and there was no point in going over all that ground once more, Kara knew. "As long as we're on the subject of flashlights," she said instead, "mine seems to be missing."

"What a shame. Maybe you can find a new one that comes with its own shoulder holster and ammunition belt."

She eyed him suspiciously. That had been an awfully prompt answer. "I don't suppose you took it, did you?"

"Nope. I might have if the idea had occurred to me," he admitted. "Purely in self-defense, you understand. But then you'd probably have armed yourself with a perfume atomizer, and on the whole, that would be worse. Midnight Passion makes me sneeze." Absolutely straight-faced, he added, "I'm speaking of the scent, you understand, not the activity."

Kara decided the only sensible course of action was to ignore him. "About Rhonda," she began. "If you want her to keep working on the bridesmaids' dresses, I'll have to tell her I'm only a temporary stand-in."

"Hold it. The fewer people who know the details of this story—"

"I understand that, and heaven knows I'm not wild about trying to explain it. But even before Anabel's little explosion tonight, Rhonda was beginning to smell week-old fish. She certainly didn't believe that everything was just peachy between the two of you."

"Why did she have a problem with that?"

Kara's voice was heavy with sarcasm. "Gee, I don't know. Maybe it's the fact that whenever she looks in this direction, you're here."

He shrugged. "We're working on wedding plans."

"Come on, Jax. She walks in to see you flat on your back on my sofa, looking as if you're about to fall asleep, and you expect her to believe we're discussing cakes and flowers?"

"It's true. Mostly, at any rate." He went on, not quite under his breath, "Only because you won't cooperate in more interesting activities, like joining me on the sofa and giving me a few good reasons to stay awake, but that's another..." He gave her a rakish glance.

Kara fought in vain to keep warm color from washing over her face. "Well, *true* isn't always the same as *credible*. More to the point, I know Rhonda won't believe the tale that since I'm simply stepping into Anabel's shoes as the substitute bride, I want to keep everything running along exactly as planned."

"Why are you so certain she won't just keep sewing? It's her job."

"Are you completely dense?" Kara had reached the end of her rope. Why, she wondered, did she bother to go on trying? "Because she knows perfectly well I don't have thirteen friends the right proportions to wear those dresses, that's why!"

"And you don't want to keep Anabel's?" Jax asked innocently. "You might become pals with every last one of them, you know, by the time this wedding is finally over."

"This wedding," Kara said, "is *never* going to be

over.'' In utter frustration, she flung a pillow at him. He caught it, hefting it thoughtfully as if considering his aim, and she reached past him to grab for more ammunition. Just as she seized the corner of the cushion Jax was leaning against, he pulled it out of her hand. Though she struggled to regain her balance, the effort was futile, and unable to catch herself, she landed on him with a thud.

Jax's arm closed around her and he leaned back farther, pulling her with him till she was sprawled full length on the sofa on top of him.

"Now this is more like it," Jax whispered. His hands wandered over her back, drawing her down till her lips were almost touching his. Every ragged breath Kara managed to draw in pressed her more tightly against him, but when she tried to stop breathing, she felt even dizzier.

Time seemed to hang suspended, measured only by the uneven skittering of her heartbeat and the confusing cacophony of voices in her head. *This is wrong*, one said. *Unwise. Doomed.*

And another answered, *This is inevitable....*

Then, just as slowly as he'd pulled her close, Jax released her, setting her upright on the sofa once more. He stood over her for a moment and let his fingertips rest briefly against her cheek. There was a strange expression in his eyes, as if he'd never seen her before. "Tomorrow," he said, and then he was gone.

Kara sat still, hugging herself and staring into the distance. What an embarrassing accident...and what sizzling consequences it could have had.

But it hadn't. For no matter how suggestive Jax had been earlier in the evening, it was apparent now that he realized physical intimacy was a complication neither of them needed.

It was certainly a complication Kara didn't want. She

was glad he'd left, she told herself, because the last thing she'd wanted to do was throw him out.

The last thing she'd wanted to do...

The double meaning echoed uncomfortably in her head. *Don't be ridiculous*, she ordered herself. She certainly hadn't wanted him to stay!

If only he hadn't looked into her eyes...

Not that he was sorry he had, exactly, Jax thought. The panic he'd seen in them had startled him, for it seemed so contradictory compared with the warmth and softness of her body melting into his. Sprawled across him as she'd been, unable even to shift her weight without increasing the intimate contact between them... But was it possible that too-convenient fall hadn't been intentional after all?

Contradictory or not, the panic in those enormous, expressive green eyes had been real, and recognizing it had been like getting a dousing with ice water.

The shock hadn't changed his goal, by any means. It had just slowed him down. Step by slow, cautious step, he'd have to regain the ground he'd lost tonight by rushing her.

He had no doubt he could do it. And ultimately, when—not if—he made love to her, panic was going to be the last thing Kara Schuyler felt.

Ultimately. That was the trouble, of course—because he didn't have all the time in the world.

Kara surveyed her entire wardrobe and finally selected a brightly flowered sundress that she hoped wouldn't be too out of place at the Montgomerys' barbecue, topping it with a crisp white linen jacket for the businesslike touch the Sloans would expect from a professional party planner.

She fussed over her makeup, telling herself how important it was to make a good impression on the Sloans this afternoon. She certainly wasn't trying to overwhelm the Montgomery family with her elegance. And as for even considering what Jax might think of her appearance...

That, she knew, would be completely crazy. It would imply that she was taking him seriously, which, in the light of his actions last night, would not only be foolish but downright stupid.

Jax had shown himself to be perfectly willing to flirt and to tease, and she had no doubt he'd have been equally as willing to indulge in casual lovemaking. Up to a certain point last night, he'd obviously been enjoying himself. What was still puzzling Kara was the question of precisely what had stopped him cold.

Of course, whatever the reason, it really didn't much matter; Kara wouldn't have let things go on much longer. She'd have to be an idiot even to consider making love with him—not only a man who in two weeks would be married to another woman, but a man who was openly using her to get that other woman back. That kind of casual lovemaking led nowhere but to—

Was that the key? Had that strange look in his eyes been the sudden realization that, unlike many other women, Kara didn't look on making love as merely a pleasant pastime? Had he suddenly feared that his fleeting pleasure wouldn't have been worthwhile in the end because she might become a nuisance, expecting far more than he was willing to give?

What a compliment it is, she thought wryly, *to know that I stand out from the crowd he's used to!*

Well, if that was what he'd been thinking, he was dead wrong. Even if she was foolish enough to want his attention—which of course she wasn't—Kara wasn't so starry-eyed as to expect anything from Jax Montgomery. And if he was so arrogant that he thought any woman who'd been around him for a couple of days must therefore cherish fond hopes of something permanent...

Well, she'd soon show him that no such thought had ever crossed her mind. If he was expecting her to be shy or coquettish, or to put on some kind of maiden act, or even to try outright to snare him, he was going to be very disappointed. She would simply be cool and at ease, as if nothing important had happened the night before—because nothing important *had* happened.

She saw the Jaguar pull into the driveway, and by the time the car stopped moving, she was standing beside it, briefcase in hand.

As Jax strolled around the car, Kara got in, settling herself carefully so the seat belt wouldn't crumple her linen jacket. When he reached her door, there was nothing left for him to do but shut it.

He didn't, however; he propped an elbow along the top of the door and looked thoughtfully down at her. "Am I late, or are you just eager to see me?"

"I'm eager to get to my appointment."

"Oh, there's plenty of time for that. And a minute left over for a hello kiss, too."

Now's the time to set the tone, Kara resolved. *Remember, nothing important happened last night, so there's no reason to act coy about kissing him.* She promptly offered her cheek and said, "Sorry, my darling. I'd have kissed you first if I'd only seen the camera. At least, I assume someone's taking pictures and that's why we're doing this?"

"Minx," he said cheerfully. His lips barely brushed her cheek.

Kara breathed a little easier. She supposed it shouldn't have been a surprise that Jax, too, would behave as if nothing had happened the night before—but it was a relief.

"When I called Mrs. Gleason this morning, she asked me to tell you hello," she said. "She somehow gathered that I'd be seeing you."

"It does appear to be a safe conclusion. Unless you didn't tell her we're engaged now?"

"Not exactly. I told her Anabel had called her in the midst of a temper tantrum and immediately regretted it, so I was trying to straighten things out."

"If that's what you call straightening—"

"What I said was at least two-thirds true. Anabel was certainly having a tantrum, and I'm the one who got stuck trying to fix the mess. Besides, for all I know, she *did* regret it, because she doesn't seem to have called everyone on the list."

"You've had a busy morning."

"I felt like I was tiptoeing through a minefield, trying to keep my stories straight."

He frowned. "What's wrong with the original one?"

"Jax, you can't have thought it through. Telling Mrs. Gleason you're supposedly engaged to me now would be a bit counterproductive if the goal is to keep her working on Anabel's dress."

"I don't see why."

"Because it's completely ludicrous to think that Mrs. Gleason would believe I'd try to wear it, that's why."

"If you're rehashing all her nonsense about which styles flatter whom—"

"It's not nonsense. Though what I'm talking about at the moment isn't style at all, it's size."

"Oh. I hadn't thought of that. But just consider what Anabel's reaction will be when she hears you're having the dress altered to fit you."

"I *am* thinking of it," Kara said grimly. "And the picture I see is Anabel laughing herself into a seizure."

The Jaguar pulled to a smooth stop at a traffic light, and Jax turned to look at Kara. "Mrs. Gleason said she could change it at the last minute."

"You needn't try to spare my feelings. What she said was she left room for expansion in case Anabel turns out to be a nervous eater right before the wedding. But she's talking a half inch here and there."

His gaze traveled thoughtfully over her. "And that's not enough to make the difference?"

"Jackson Montgomery, you are not inexperienced enough to overlook the discrepancies between Anabel's figure and mine."

He shrugged. "I suppose there are a few—"

"The fact is, Anabel is roughly the shape of the Washington Monument—really tall and very slim. I'm more like..." Kara fumbled for a comparison that would drill home the difference without making her sound totally dumpy next to the beauty queen.

"The Jefferson Memorial," Jax offered helpfully. "Nicely rounded."

"Thanks—I think. The point is that there's nothing really wrong with either one, but they're never going to change places. Anyway, I had to promise to stop by to see Mrs. Gleason tomorrow so I can check on the dress myself. But if you have any suggestions how I can explain to her that Anabel won't be dropping in for the last round of fittings any time soon—"

"If we time the visit right, there might be cream puffs," he said hopefully.

"Who said you were invited to come along? I only asked if you had any suggestions."

"All right," Jax said equably. "If you don't want my support in convincing Mrs. Gleason to keep working—"

"The only thing you're planning to support is the weight of a cream puff between the plate and your mouth," Kara accused.

"Wrong on two counts. There *is* no weight to Mrs. Gleason's cream puffs, and—"

"Jax, the light's green."

"And I wouldn't stop at one." The car behind them honked impatiently, and finally he stopped watching Kara and turned his attention back to the road. "Besides, I thought we might play golf with a couple of my cousins tomorrow, so we wouldn't be free to make calls till mid-afternoon anyway."

"I don't play golf."

It was, she thought, the first time she'd ever seen him astonished. "You *are* joking. I know you took lessons because—"

Kara winced and, before he had a chance to, said, "Because in your caddie days, you were one of the unlucky souls who had to retrieve the golf balls after I had a session on the driving range. Don't remind me."

"Now that I think of it—"

"I didn't make those wild shots just to annoy you, you know."

"You're cutting me to the heart, Kara Jo," he murmured. "I was certain you did it purely to get my attention. Anyway, just consider how romantic everybody will think it is when you walk the course with me tomorrow because you can't bear to be separated for four hours."

"When I want a walk," Kara said firmly, "I'll go for a walk. And I won't be chasing a little white golf ball."

"You're firm on that? No golf?" He sounded disappointed.

Good, Kara thought. That meant she'd made her point quite plainly enough, and now she'd have four whole hours tomorrow when she could relax her guard. "Absolutely none."

"Well, I'm sure my cousins will understand." The Jaguar slowed and turned into a driveway, pausing before an elaborate set of gates. "They'll be able to play faster as a twosome anyway, so they might get in two rounds." He lowered the window and pressed an intercom button near the gate.

They had reached the Sloan estate—and Kara had been so intent on Jax that she hadn't even done a last-minute review of what she intended to say. Everything she'd prepared seemed to have flown straight out of her mind.

"As a twosome?" she heard herself say. "But surely you—"

The intercom crackled. Jax gave her name, and the gates swung slowly open. As the Jaguar crept through, he said, "If you won't play golf so you can be with me, then I won't play, either, so I can be with you. The only question is what we should do instead. I'm sure—expert that you are, Kara Jo—you can think of something really romantic."

With the interview over, Kara waited for the Sloans' elegant gates to click shut behind them before she sagged in the Jaguar's seat and stared wide-eyed at Jax. "I can't believe you did that!"

"What?" He sounded completely innocent.

"All of it. Starting with getting out of the car and introducing yourself as my briefcase bearer—and thanks very much for not letting me know ahead of time that you came along because I have a bad back and can't pick it up by myself. Do you have any idea how many things I lift for the average party?''

"No, and if you're worried that I made you look like a weakling, I'll bet Mrs. Sloan doesn't have a clue, either. Besides, I'm sure your back will be much better by the time Emily Sloan actually turns sweet sixteen.''

"I thought we'd agreed that you were going to wait in the car.''

"You did ask for my help,'' he reminded her. "How was I going to be helpful sitting out in the broiling sun?''

"I changed my mind—remember?''

"You have to admit when Donald started to get restless, I was the one who saved the day.''

"Which is another thing I can't believe. Out of all the topics on earth, you had to ask him why men get so attached to their razors!''

"That's not exactly what I asked him. And I happen to think it was an excellent choice. Razors are his main product, and I've never met a CEO yet, recluse or not, who didn't want to talk about his product.'' He reached for her hand, lying tense on the seat between them, and squeezed it. "Come on, Kara Jo. What does it matter what the subject was? He relaxed, didn't he? And you came out of it with not only the sweet-sixteen party but a fundraiser to do.''

"Oh, yes, that's yet one more thing I can't believe you did. 'Kara's an expert at these charity affairs,''' she mimicked.

"What's the problem? You told me yourself you're good at it.''

"So good that I don't need any help getting more worthy causes, thanks very much. Especially ones in desperate need of large infusions of cash within the month.''

He looked a little chastened. "A month? I missed that part. That's going to put a little pressure on you, isn't it?"

"*A little*? And did you have to suggest that I present a plan for both these events next weekend?"

"Well, I can't go with you midweek to distract Donald."

"Thanks a lot. Since you're the one who got me into the fund-raiser mess, I don't suppose you'd like to take me off the hook by just writing a check? Don't bother answering—I know better."

"It did seem like a good cause."

"They all do," Kara said wearily. "Don't worry about making your contribution. As soon as I figure out how to raise the money, I'll put you to work."

"Don't forget I'll be on my honeymoon."

"You have to manage to get married first."

"You know," Jax said thoughtfully, "that's a very interesting problem. You're the one who suggested I have a bachelor party and a reception without an actual wedding, so why couldn't I—"

Kara raised her voice. "As long as we're speaking of contributions—"

"I thought we'd switched to honeymoons."

"—I promised Rhonda I'd get her an advance this weekend. And it wouldn't hurt to make a payment to Mrs. Gleason, either."

"It might help her overlook the little flaws in your story," Jax agreed.

"*My* story?"

"Unfortunately, I don't have my checkbook with me at the moment."

"Why am I not surprised?" Kara muttered.

"Which means I'll have to come with you tomorrow, doesn't it?"

Kara put her head back against the leather seat. "If I'd had any idea how impossible you are—"

"You'd have taken your flashlight and gone home, I suppose," Jax said. "And just think what you'd be missing now."

Turmoil, trauma and tall tales, Kara told herself. *That's right—just think what I'd be missing!*

CHAPTER SEVEN

KARA leaned back in the lounge chair and looked up through the widespread branches of the giant oak tree to the indigo sky. Jeannette Montgomery's barbecue was drawing to a close, but a burst of laughter, the murmur of conversation and the clink of glasses still formed a pleasant background pattern.

It was a very good thing, Kara told herself, that she hadn't wasted any time beforehand speculating on what Jax's extended family might be like. In a million years, she'd never have anticipated the Montgomerys....

Jax nudged her feet aside so he could perch on the end of the chair. "What are you doing over here by yourself?" he asked.

Kara didn't move. "I'm recuperating from the strain."

"What strain? They like you."

She raised her head enough to stare at him. "Jax, you must have noticed the strange looks."

"Of course I have," he said cheerfully. "I know Uncle Albert has what is sometimes euphemistically referred to as a Roman nose, and that Cousin Eleanor—"

"I meant the strange looks they were giving me. It must have been your Aunt Agnes who looked me up and down over the tops of her glasses and said, 'The standards for beauty queens have changed since my day.' And somebody named Ruth said, 'But, dear, that was the other one. This is Jax's *new* fiancée' and they both went straight on as if it was a perfectly normal conversation."

"Doesn't sound so strange to me. Aunt Agnes always

could put both feet in her mouth and never even notice that she'd done it.''

Kara sighed. ''Are your family events always like this?''

''Aren't everybody's?''

''I have never in my life experienced anything like this.''

''Really? What were your family gatherings like?''

What family gatherings? she almost said. Or, which was almost equally true, *What family*? She drew a painfully deep breath and said levelly, ''You knew my grandparents.''

He didn't answer, but he reached for her hand, and she saw a softness in his eyes. She didn't want to look too closely; it would be difficult enough to know that he was sympathetic, but unbearable if he was to feel pity.

Quickly, she said, ''Do me a favor, Jax?''

''Anything within reason, princess.''

''You always leave yourself a back door, don't you?'' she mused. ''When all this is over between you and me, and your mother throws another barbecue in order to introduce Anabel to the Montgomery clan, would you ask her to invite me?''

''Sure. Bet you can't wait to meet up with Aunt Agnes again.''

''I want to see Anabel's face. That's all. I'll just stand in a corner—assuming I can find one—and watch quietly. You know, if anybody had told me your mother could put sixty-seven people, including a dozen kids under the age of five, into a backyard the size of a handkerchief—''

''It's a whole lot bigger than that,'' Jax objected. ''Believe me, I know, because I used to be the one who had to mow it.''

''I'll concede the square footage if you'll admit it was

practically standing room only. And yet there were no lost tempers and no injured feelings—''

''We've all gotten used to Aunt Agnes, you see.''

''Well, it just surprised me.'' She looked around at the well-trampled lawn, the simple cedar deck and the plain, straight lines of the ranch-style house. ''All of it.''

''You expected by now I'd have moved them into a new glass-and-steel monstrosity up the street from the Century Club?''

Kara's gaze drifted across the mismatched assortment of tables and chairs, mostly empty now, which had accommodated the crowd. Jeannette was gathering up packets of photographs that had been passed around all afternoon; her husband came up behind her and bent to kiss the nape of her neck.

''Maybe not glass and steel,'' Kara said, ''but I expected the sun king would have tried something of the sort.''

''I did. Mom told me I must have a better use for my money, and Dad said he knew every wiring splice and plumbing joint in this whole house because he's repaired most of them, and he wasn't interested in starting to learn a new one.''

''All of which means they're just sentimental. And apparently not just about houses.'' Kara felt like a voyeur, but she couldn't stop looking at the Montgomerys. Jeannette had turned in her husband's arms and was smiling up at him.

Jax glanced over his shoulder, following her gaze. ''They'll have been married thirty-five years next March, and they're still carrying on like that.'' His voice was lazy.

Kara said wistfully, ''I think it's sweet.'' She saw the sudden lift of his eyebrows and hurried on before he could point out how naive she must have sounded. "Shouldn't we go pitch in to clear up the mess?"

"Mom hires a crew of the neighborhood kids."

"Oh. Well, I wouldn't want to cheat somebody out of a job."

"Good thinking. The night is young—let's do something fun."

"Like what?" Too late, Kara saw a familiar gleam spring to life in his eyes and realized she'd left herself wide open to any seductive suggestion he cared to make. "I have an idea," she added hastily. "I just remembered that we haven't done anything all day to annoy Anabel. In public, I mean."

She thought he was trying very hard to look disappointed at her quick recovery, though the twinkle of humor insisted on coming through. His voice, however, was sober. "That's very true. We haven't." Jax stood and, with one effortless motion, pulled her to her feet. "And it would be such a shame to miss the opportunity."

The Montgomerys had moved into the house; in the kitchen, Kara hugged Jeannette and said, "I'd be happy to stay and help clean up."

"Dear child," Jeannette said, "*I'm* not going to stick around to watch the process, so I guarantee you'd only be in the way."

"I told you," Jax murmured, and drew her on through the house.

In the living room, a couple of young men—Jax's cousins, Kara thought, though she couldn't remember the names—had settled in to watch the sports channel. One of them looked up. "Where are you off to?"

"A nightclub called Glitterati," Jax said genially. "Not that it matters much, because you're not invited to come along."

The young man laughed. "Enjoy yourself. But don't think we won't drag you out of bed in the morning to make our tee time."

"I was going to tell you—" Jax began.

"I'll send him home early tonight, I promise," Kara said quickly. "I know he couldn't bear to miss his golf date." She shot a pseudo bashful look up at Jax. "I realize you would've skipped it for my sake, darling, but I just couldn't ask you to make the sacrifice."

Jax snorted.

"Now that," his cousin said, "is a woman to hang on to, Jax."

Kara was giggling as they walked out to his car.

"A woman to hang on to," Jax muttered. "That's true enough—and sometimes it feels like the appropriate grip would be around your neck."

"Don't be silly. You know you'll enjoy the morning much more playing golf than you would hanging around and annoying me." Kara had already moved on to other concerns. "It would have to be Glitterati, wouldn't it?" The city's newest, most glamorous and most sophisticated nightclub. She should have expected that Anabel would have settled for nothing less since Glitterati was the stylish place to be seen.

"Something wrong with that? It was your idea."

"Only that if I'd been thinking, I'd have realized that of course Glitterati would be Anabel's favorite place."

Jax gave her a sharp glance.

A bit too late, Kara remembered that it might be prudent to watch what she said about Anabel. She'd been getting careless, she realized, too quick to voice what she thought. But the fact that Jax hadn't been jumping to the woman's defense at the slightest hint of a slur didn't mean that his loyalties weren't aroused; it probably just indicated that so far he hadn't thought Kara's opinions were important enough to quarrel with. But there was a point, she suspected, beyond which a wise woman wouldn't push him.

Worse, he was arrogant enough to assume that she was simply being catty, that she considered herself in some sort of weird competition with Anabel—with Jax as the prize. And she'd really rather not prompt him to think anything of the sort.

Not only was there no substance for that suspicion, but giving him any cause for conceit would only cause trouble in the short run and likely be one more untidy loose end to trip over before this was finished.

She explained, almost mildly, "I just meant that I'm dressed for a barbecue, not the most exotic spot in town."

"Give your hair a shake and put on some fresh lipstick and you'll be fine."

"Right. Men have it so easy."

There was a crush on the sidewalk outside the nightclub, but Glitterati's doorman greeted Jax with enthusiasm. "Miss Randall hasn't been in this evening," he said.

"What a pity." Jax drew Kara apart from the crowd and tucked her hand more tightly into the crook of his elbow.

The doorman, recognizing the connection between them an instant too late, flushed purple with embarrassment. "I mean—"

"Never mind, Henry." Jax stepped through the door into the loudest music Kara had ever heard.

If you can really call it music, she thought. "That's too bad," she shouted into Jax's ear. "The doorman, I mean. If Anabel shows up, he won't even tell her we've been here. He'll only turn beet-red and look guilty."

"There's more to Glitterati's grapevine than just

Henry. What do you want to drink? And where would you like to sit?''

A nice cup of hot chocolate, in my bed with a book, Kara wanted to say. Not that she'd get what she wanted, and in this noise Jax would probably hear only a random word or two—probably the more suggestive ones at that. ''Ginger ale,'' she replied in her loudest voice. ''And as far from the band as we can.''

He grinned and pointed out a table in the most distant corner, and the hostess nodded and ushered them over to it. Kara's head was beginning to throb from the noise even before their drinks arrived, and she could hardly hear his question.

''What do you think of Glitterati?''

''It's a great place for a first date,'' Kara shouted. ''Nobody has to talk!''

Me and my big mouth, she berated herself. Even though she hadn't exactly had Glitterati in mind, it had been her suggestion to try out Anabel's favorite haunts. Why hadn't it occurred to her that Anabel's sort of place was likely to be noisy and stuffed full of people just like the beauty queen, wanting to see and be seen?

It was probably a waste of time, too, Kara thought as she glanced around the room. Between the dim lighting and the occasional flare of mood-setting strobes, she couldn't identify anyone in the press of bodies if they were more than six feet off. Even if Anabel had been in the club, she could be sitting just three tables away and never see them.

Kara was waiting for a momentary drop in the decibel level so she could point that out to Jax when a wave of familiar perfume assaulted her.

Jax pushed his chair back and rose, but Anabel hardly looked at him; her furious gaze was focused on Kara instead. She leaned over the table, and Kara smothered a gasp and hoped that Anabel's strapless black leather dress wouldn't slip. But it seemed to have been glued in place.

Kara heard herself say, "Henry told us you hadn't been in."

"Henry who? Not that I care." Anabel glared at the diamond on Kara's left hand. "I know exactly what you're up to."

Congratulations, Sherlock Holmes, Kara wanted to say. *Now can I go home and let you and Jax work it all out?* "Good. You can stop trying to cancel the wedding, and I—"

"And you can stop giving me orders. You're not going to get away with this." Anabel's low voice was hard and husky as she turned to Jax. "I don't know what kind of dirt she's got on you, Jax, but I'm not giving up till I find out exactly how she's blackmailing you."

Her gaze flicked challengingly over Kara once more, and seconds later she was lost in the crowd.

Kara's ears were ringing. "Now that's devotion," she said hopefully. "She's obviously worried about you, and—"

"Jumping to the conclusion that I'm being blackmailed is not precisely a ringing endorsement." Jax settled back into his seat. "And she also didn't sound much like a woman who's ready to stop trying to manage my life."

Kara couldn't exactly argue with that. Anabel hadn't sounded willing to negotiate, much less surrender—and Jax was unlikely to accept anything else.

Her head hurt, and not only because of Glitterati's music. It had been three days since Anabel's original blowup, and Kara had had every reason to hope that by now things would be well on their way to being straightened out.

Instead, the whole situation was growing murkier with every passing moment.

On Sunday morning, still nursing the remains of her noise-induced headache, Kara settled down with a fresh cup of coffee and a clean notebook and started to doodle, trying to brainstorm plans for Emily Sloan's sweet-sixteen party.

Normally, for a party that was still three months in the future, she would simply drop the subject into her subconscious for a couple of weeks, and when she eventually sat down to plan, the ideas would almost magically appear. But this time, she didn't have that luxury since Jax had as much as told the Sloans that she'd have a preliminary scheme ready to present next weekend.

What had the man been thinking of? It was almost as if he'd been trying to get himself invited back—

Abruptly, she realized that she was thinking about Jax again, and not the parties at all.

She reached for yet another notebook, one that would be devoted to the fund-raiser for Mrs. Sloan's amateur theater group. The first question, she supposed, was what kinds of activity could raise lots of money in a very short time. The kind of events that raised enormous amounts of cash usually required a corresponding amount of planning and capital investment. The last big charity event she'd been involved in had taken six months to schedule, arrange and finance. It was too bad that more casual events simply weren't able to raise enough money to be worthwhile. Things like plays and variety shows that the theater group could do by itself. Or things like barbecues...

Not that Jeannette Montgomery's barbecue had been a simple affair, of course. The fact that it had ended up looking perfectly easy was the mark, Kara knew, of good planning and early preparation by a hostess who was perfectly at ease.

Jeannette Montgomery, Kara felt, had more class in her left eyebrow than most people had in total. And the closeness and love she'd observed between Jeannette and her husband made Kara's heart ache every time she thought about it.

She wondered idly if the Montgomerys would consider adopting her—all the Montgomerys, except for Jax, of course.

Jax the incorrigible. The fact that he could watch a demonstration of his parents' affection and make a smart remark about it illustrated his lack of understanding. Evidently, he didn't have the slightest idea how rare John and Jeannette Montgomery were—thirty-five years married and still so obviously in love...

In all probability, that lack of understanding might go a long way toward explaining his attitude toward Anabel. Come to that, Kara had discovered for herself that he wasn't much for compromise and negotiation.

The doorbell rang and Kara sighed, wondering if it was possible Jax was already done with his round of golf or if he'd skipped it after all.

But it was Rhonda at the door instead. Kara brought her a cup of coffee and they settled at the breakfast bar in the comfortable silence of good friends.

Finally, Rhonda said, ''The courier service delivered that last bolt of satin this morning. You know—the expensive one.''

''On Sunday?''

''When you pay enough, anything's possible.''

''Ouch,'' Kara conceded. ''I'll get the money, Rhonda.''

"I wasn't dunning you, exactly. I just wondered what I'm supposed to do with the fabric now it's here."

"Make a bridesmaid's dress," Kara said lightly.

"To fit Anabel's thirteenth bridesmaid—the one with the figure of a paper doll?"

"Right."

"Even though the sun king's hanging around here all the time and you're suddenly wearing a rock the size of Mount Rushmore?"

"They're putting the darnedest things in breakfast cereal these days as premium prizes."

"Very good," Rhonda said. "That wasn't a lie. Quite." She sighed. "Kara, I don't have the foggiest what you're up to, but I'm afraid you're getting in way over your head."

Believe me, Kara thought, *I know.*

When Jax hadn't shown up by midafternoon, Kara told herself it was insane to wait for him as if she had nothing better to do. If he came after such a long delay, the fact that she was sitting around twiddling her thumbs would only feed an ego that was already in no danger of being malnourished. And if he didn't come at all, she'd have not only wasted an entire day but broken her promise to Mrs. Gleason, as well.

She dug a basket from the cupboard and began to pack it with delicacies to take to the old lady.

Perhaps, she reflected, despite Jax's firmness last night, he'd had second thoughts and sought out Anabel today, and the two of them were working things out....

The very idea should have been a comfort, providing the hope that the mess would soon be over and she could stop feeling as if she were picking her way across quicksand. Instead, trying to picture Jax and Anabel actually negotiating their differences only made her feel flat and depressed.

Because it's about as likely as a greyhound winning the Kentucky Derby, she thought. *He'll only settle for surrender.*

That attitude didn't say much for the eventual success of the marriage—but that was hardly Kara's business. Once Anabel capitulated and the wedding was over, Jax—and Anabel, of course—would no longer be any concern of Kara's.

I can hardly wait, she told herself grimly, and reached for her keys. It was long past time to stop hanging around the house and go visit Mrs. Gleason.

When she knocked, Mrs. Gleason's cheery voice called, "It's open!"

Kara gave the door a push. "Mrs. Gleason, you know how much it worries me when you leave your door unlocked."

"Now, dear," the woman said placidly. She didn't even look up from the folds of white satin spread across her lap, and her fingers didn't pause. "The doorman will be careful not to let any murderers into the building."

"I'm sure he will, as long as they tell him what they're planning to do, but…" Kara stopped dead on the threshold as Jax rose from the only comfortable chair in Mrs. Gleason's living room.

He wasn't with Anabel. He was here.

Merely seeing him made her heart race. How odd, she thought, that he hadn't stopped by the duplex so they could come together.…

And how silly, she mocked herself, *to think any such thing!* He didn't need either Kara's permission to visit Mrs. Gleason or her guidance in order to find the way.

She kept her voice light. "This is a surprise."

"It certainly is," Jax said. "I assumed you were coming this morning."

She could almost read his mind. *Since you worked so hard to get rid of me.* "And how was your golf game?" Kara asked sweetly.

"Not much better than yours would've been. I was distracted, you see. I kept thinking of you—" His voice had gone husky.

Don't even listen to him, she told herself. But that sensual undertone made her throat feel tight.

Jax finished. "—Sitting here eating cream puffs without me."

"My goodness," Mrs. Gleason said, "I'd almost forgotten to offer you tea."

Kara rolled her eyes. "Montgomery, you should be ashamed of yourself. That was such a heavy hint I'm surprised you didn't need a crane to move it."

Mrs. Gleason sounded placid. "Everything's ready in the kitchen, Kara, if you wouldn't mind making the tea. I'm in the middle of a motif, and my hands cramp when I've been sewing for a while. Perhaps Mr. Montgomery will carry in the tea tray."

"Good idea. Jax would hate it if anybody dropped the cream puffs, so we'll make it his responsibility." Kara looked at the pile of satin in Mrs. Gleason's lap. "It's obvious you've hardly put down your needle lately. I didn't think it was possible you could be so far along yet."

"Oh, Mr. Montgomery has impressed on me how important it is that this dress not be delayed." Mrs. Gleason's eyes twinkled as she looked up at him.

"Persuasive, isn't he?" Kara muttered. Just inside the kitchen, she stopped to look up at him with narrowed eyes.

"What now?" Jax sounded defensive. "You said you wanted me to convince her to keep working. If you're expecting me to explain how I did it..."

Kara turned the heat up under the kettle and put her basket of goodies on the counter. "I'm not sure I want to know."

"Good—because I wasn't going to tell you anyway." His eyes lit up. "Look at that tray."

The treats Mrs. Gleason had laid out made the contents of Kara's basket look meager. Chocolate-covered macadamia nuts, dainty cookies, smoked salmon sandwiches...

"What did she do? Pull an armed robbery of a gourmet shop?" Kara felt like tucking her contributions away in the farthest corner of the kitchen to avoid comparison with this bounty.

"She probably learned the technique from you," Jax murmured. "I bet *that's* where your flashlight went. Mrs. Gleason lifted it to use in her holdup."

Kara ignored him and made the tea. Back in the living room, she set the teapot down on the small table nearest Mrs. Gleason's chair and said, "I've never seen so many goodies on one tray in my life."

Mrs. Gleason reached for another handful of beads. "Isn't it wonderful? A deliveryman from that big store over on Jackson Avenue brought a nice box of things just yesterday."

Kara glanced at Jax. He looked almost too innocent. "With no card, of course."

"Oh, no, dear—with the compliments of the store manager. I never knew before that they sent out samples to prospective customers." Mrs. Gleason frowned a little. "I wouldn't think they could afford it, though, giving things away like that. It really was an enormous box."

"Oh, they do it all the time," Kara said dryly. "The

way banks give out sample hundred-dollar bills to every customer who comes in. As long as we're talking of money—''

''I wondered how long it would take you to come around to that.'' Jax was hungrily eyeing the tea tray.

''You did say you'd bring your checkbook today. So—''

The old woman clicked her tongue. ''Now, Kara. Money is such an unpleasant topic. Besides, Mr. Montgomery already dealt with that before you arrived, so there's nothing more to talk about. Do try the smoked salmon, dear.''

Since it was apparent she intended to say no more, Kara subsided, biting her tongue and reminding herself that in the final analysis, the financial arrangements were none of her affair. She was the coordinator, not the boss, and if Mrs. Gleason was satisfied with the payment Jax had offered—whatever it was—then the amount really wasn't Kara's concern.

If only the woman wasn't quite so trusting when it came to business deals...

She was only half following the conversation, and a little later when Jax rose to say goodbye, Kara was almost too startled to act. ''Surely you can't be leaving so soon,'' she said. ''There are still a couple of cream puffs left on the tray.'' She hastily said her own farewells and walked out with him, stopping on the sidewalk in front of the apartment building. ''All right, you successfully sidetracked me where Mrs. Gleason's concerned. But you still owe Rhonda money, too—and a whole lot of other people.''

''And here I thought you were in such a hurry to come along because after a morning apart you realized you can't bear to be separated from me.'' He pulled a leather folder from his pocket and waved it under her nose. "Here it is. One checkbook, as promised."

"Good. The stack of bills is in my car."

"So you were hoping to see me after all," Jax murmured. "Or you wouldn't have brought them along."

Kara refused to take the bait. "Are you coming?"

"Wouldn't you rather sit somewhere more comfortable than your car? I would. The trouble is—"

"I ought to have known there would be some."

"We have two vehicles. If we leave one here while we go out for coffee, it'll probably be towed for overtime parking. And the Jaguar's almost out of fuel, so my first stop will have to be—"

"My place, half an hour." Kara sighed. Then before he could move, she extracted the checkbook from his hand and tucked it into her purse. "Just so you won't get delayed, I'll keep custody of this in the meantime."

Instead of the protest she'd half expected, Jax smiled. "Good. You can go ahead and write all the checks. The part about who gets paid, I mean. There may still be some discussion of amounts."

"What a surprise *that* is," Kara muttered.

As soon as she got home, she started the coffeemaker brewing and spread out her assortment of bills on her worktable. Reimbursing Rhonda for those ghastly delivery charges was the top priority, of course. She found her calculator and Rhonda's receipts, then reached for Jax's checkbook.

It fell open to a list of the most recent checks he'd written, and in the long row of names, her own caught her eye. *That's odd*, she thought. *I've never gotten a check from Jax, just from Anabel*. But there she was....

Not as a payee, however, she realized. Her name was simply noted off to the side as the ultimate recipient; the check had been made out to Anabel—for fifteen thousand dollars.

She stared at the entry for a full minute, trying to make sense of it. Then, knowing full well she was snooping, she paged back through the past few months' entries.

There were three more entries, identical except for the amounts. In the past eight weeks, Jax had written checks to Anabel for a total of forty-five thousand dollars, noting that part of the money was for Kara herself, part to pass along to the caterer, the photographer, the florist.

Forty-five thousand dollars—and Kara had seen almost none of it.

She felt as if she'd taken a left hook out of nowhere. No wonder Jax had been so consistently unsympathetic about paying the outstanding bills for this wedding; he believed he'd already paid—and paid very well indeed.

When he knocked at the back door minutes later, Kara was still staring at the checkbook. She put it down and let him in.

"I still think your garage looks more like a spaceship lab," Jax said, and paused. "What's the matter?"

Kara tried to wet her lips. "No wonder you haven't been eager to pay the bills." Her voice was flat, lifeless. "And no wonder you thought it was my responsibility instead."

"You might consider giving me a few more details so I can join this conversation."

"Anabel told you I was paying everybody." She stared up at him. "And when I told you they hadn't been paid, you thought I'd just tucked the excess under my mattress. Didn't you?"

"The idea occurred to me."

She swallowed hard. "You don't really think the average wedding planner gets paid fifteen thousand dollars up front as a retainer before she ever does a stroke of work, do you?''

"Nobody ever said you were ordinary, Kara Jo."

Her voice cracked. "This isn't a joke."

"I wasn't laughing much myself. How should I know what wedding planners cost—or weddings, for that matter?"

"I wouldn't exactly call this a budget wedding. But Anabel hasn't paid out anywhere close to forty-five thousand dollars. She certainly didn't pass on that kind of money to me."

He merely looked at her, eyebrows slightly lifted.

"Dammit, Jax, Anabel was embezzling from you!" Suddenly, she was desperate for him to understand. "You wrote checks to her, she cashed them and wrote much smaller ones—to me and directly to the suppliers. *She's* the one who kept the rest."

"I don't suppose you can prove that."

"I can show you the actual bills she paid, plus my bank records, where I deposited the checks she gave me. I suppose you'll say I manipulated that—"

"There are ways."

"But why would I have faked anything? If I was skimming money, how could I possibly have anticipated that you'd ever catch on?"

"Common sense," Jax said dryly.

"But who would have guessed that Anabel would break your engagement? If it wasn't for that, she'd still be covering up—and asking for more. Did she actually fake receipts to show you, or did she just bat her big brown eyes when she told you that I needed another fifteen thousand here and there?"

"Kara—"

"I wonder what she did with the money...no, that's a

stupid question. It's obvious what she did with it. Anabel's a pretty high-maintenance project. What I really wonder is what she intended to do about the rest of the bills. Tell you the wedding cost even more than she'd expected? And how much more could she have gotten away with—'' She stopped abruptly. Jax looked somber, she thought. Almost grim.

"I think," Jax said coolly, "that you should quit speculating, sit down and get control of yourself."

Kara gulped, realizing too late that wildly accusing Anabel was no way to establish her own credibility. "I'm sorry. I shouldn't have said all that. I don't know how to prove I'm telling the truth, Jax. But I swear to you…" Her voice was trembling and her knees were shaky.

He guided her onto one of the high stools by the breakfast bar and started opening cabinet doors till he located the coffee mugs. Putting a cup in front of her, he sat down across the breakfast bar with one of his own.

He looked abstracted, as if his thoughts were a thousand miles away.

Great move, Kara, she told herself. *Pass the buck. And in the process, make yourself look even guiltier. If you have to trash Anabel to make yourself look decent…*

She stared at the steam rising off her coffee; she felt too clumsy even to try to drink it.

"You know," Jax said, "maybe it's for the best."

She sneaked a wary look at him. "You sound awfully cheerful about it."

"I'm not happy about the money—"

"Well, of course," Kara said before she could stop herself. "What else could possibly be bothering you?" She gritted her teeth, hard.

But Jax hadn't seemed to hear her. "In the long run, though, it appears I got off relatively cheaply. Just think what she could have done to my finances if she'd had free access.''

Kara almost dropped her coffee. "You were actually going to give her *free access*? Sorry, it's none of my business. But I'd have thought it was obvious that Anabel would be pretty much a walletful even for a gazillion-aire." She thought better of it and tried again. "I'll get to work first thing tomorrow."

"Doing what?" Jax's voice was casual.

"Canceling. Saving you what money I still can—"

"Why?"

"Please, Jax, you're giving me a headache. There's no choice now. You'll have to bite the bullet, pay the cancellation fees and—"

"Of course there's a choice."

"You can't mean you want to go on with the wedding. What is it with you and Anabel anyway—an addiction? Now that you know what she's capable of—"

"I didn't say anything about Anabel."

"Well, you can't have a wedding without a..." She saw him start to smile, and her voice trailed off.

"Fiancée?" Jax said gently. "But I have one, darling."

Kara's head was spinning.

"Think about it," he went on reasonably. "The main thing Anabel really had going for her was the whole beauty-queen image."

Momentarily, Kara was relieved. "I'm certainly no competition there."

"But beauty—intriguing though it is—doesn't always last. The Schuyler name, on the other hand, will maintain its value forever. When it comes right down to it, for my purposes you're even better than Anabel would be. A toast," Jax said, and held up his coffee cup. "To Kara Montgomery. To my wife."

CHAPTER EIGHT

KARA stared at him for a full minute, and then she shook her head. "Oh, no, you don't. You're not going to trip me up with that kind of trick."

"I assure you—" Jax's voice was silky.

"I grant it wasn't a bad idea, to try to shock me into giving myself away and admitting I'm the guilty party after all. But since I don't have the cash, and I never did, I can't throw myself on your mercy with a confession, much less offer to pay it all back."

"Slow down, Kara. This isn't a trick, you know."

"Of course it is." *It can't be anything else.* She was having trouble getting a full breath, but she plunged on regardless. "So what's the next threat? If I continue to stand firm and swear I don't have your money, you'll call the police and tell them you've suddenly remembered that I kidnapped you after all?"

"Thanks for reminding me of that little incident," Jax said calmly.

Kara could have bitten her tongue off. She scrambled to regain her position. "Well, you won't do that, and I know it. You won't ever publicly accuse me of being a kidnapper because you'd make yourself a laughingstock."

His tone was thoughtful. "In the light of these new circumstances, however, I might be able to make something of it."

She couldn't for the life of her see what. But that wasn't much comfort; she hadn't anticipated this screwball reaction to Anabel's embezzlement, so why should she expect to predict the way Jax would handle anything else? "I swear I never got that money."

"I believe you."

She went straight on. "If I had, why would I even have approached you? It would have been apparent that—what did you say?"

"You might have given it a try," Jax said dispassionately. "But as soon as you saw that the scam wasn't going to play any longer, you'd have promptly bailed out—if you'd had the cash to do it. So the only conclusion is that you didn't have the cash."

Piqued by the less-than-flattering appraisal, Kara snapped, "You're right about that much. I'd happily hand over the last cent of it just to get out of this nightmare." She shook her head a little, half-relieved—at least he'd said he believed her—but more puzzled than ever. "But if you know I didn't cheat you, why threaten me like this?"

"That's an interesting way to describe a marriage proposal," Jax mused. "I told you. The Schuyler name—"

"Names aren't everything. Let me tell you about the Schuylers, and I bet you decide you don't want them."

A smile tugged at the corner of Jax's mouth. "I'm really only interested in one," he pointed out.

"The one who treated you like dirt." Things were starting to come clear. "Now we're finally getting down to it, aren't we? You've been watching for an opportunity to get even with me for the stupid things I did years ago when I was nothing but a silly and thoughtless teenager—"

"By marrying you," Jax said mildly.

"By *threatening* to marry me. You're only dangling the sword over my head for a while in order to punish me for the way I accidentally humiliated you all those years ago.''

''Accidentally?''

''You don't think I did it on purpose, do you? I hardly even knew you existed back then.'' She paused for a moment. *Telling him he wasn't even important enough to insult is not the way to make things better.*

''Tell me again who you think is supposed to be getting punished here, Kara. I seem to have lost track.''

''Exactly. That's how I know you're only making idle threats —because it would hurt you more than me if you really went through with it.''

''Okay.'' Jax shrugged. ''So call my bluff.''

''You mean—agree to marry you?''

''If you're so sure I'm only tormenting you, then the next logical step is to think that the moment you accept my proposal, I'll stammer and stumble around and run for the door.''

Jax? Stammering and stumbling? Hardly. When he headed for the door, he'd be a lot smoother about it than that. But the results would be the same, of course. So...

Kara opened her mouth to tell him, with all the insincerity she could muster, that she'd absolutely love to be his wife. But the words seemed to stick in her throat.

''What's the matter?'' he asked gently. ''If you're afraid, down deep, that I'm not bluffing after all...''

She tried to swallow the rock in her throat.

''You should trust your instincts,'' he went on relentlessly. ''Because there are much more effective ways to get even than to make idle threats.''

''At least you're admitting that you want to get even.'' Her voice was little more than a whisper.

Jax shook his head. ''This has nothing to do with history, Kara Jo.''

"Would you stop calling me that?"

"Why? Because your grandmother did? It's not what happened then that's important. It's what you are now."

"What I am now? I'm furious and upset and—"

"I'd prefer to call you slightly reluctant. But I seem to remember that's the proper behavior for a young woman of good family when she receives a proposal. She's supposed to be a little diffident as well as modest, demure—"

"You want *demure*? Forget it, Montgomery!" Kara picked up the nearest object—his checkbook—and flung it at him as hard as she could.

He fielded it neatly. "Pretending to be surprised by the gentleman's interest..."

Kara wished she'd thrown her coffee mug. "You've gone completely bananas, you know. Your disappointment with Anabel has sent you over the edge."

"No—it's just made me look around at alternatives."

"But that's not a fit way to look at marriage! To coldly calculate the advantages to be gained from—"

"It's been done for generations in all the best families."

A stray thought floated through Kara's mind. *I wonder if my grandparents' marriage was arranged for them....* She shook it away. "You're settling for so much less than you could have. Look at your parents, Jax—"

"I do, frequently."

"Don't you want that for yourself? The love, the warmth, the comfort, the ease they so obviously have together?"

"Sure. But let's be realistic for a moment. How many people walk up the aisle thinking they're getting that sort of bliss? And how many people actually do?"

"Precisely none of the ones who approach the whole question from the direction you've chosen," Kara said crisply. "But there's really no point in discussing this further. I'm canceling the wedding."

Jax finished his coffee and set his cup down with a click. "No, you're not."

"I'm certainly not going through with it."

He didn't answer, just looked at her and smiled.

The confidence in his eyes and the caress of that knowing smile made Kara feel shaky all the way to the core, and she had to exert effort to say, "It's less than two weeks away, Jax. The longer you wait, the more expensive it'll be to get out of this."

"For one of us. Do you care to bet which one it ends up being?" His voice was very soft.

He came around the breakfast bar to stand beside her, one arm lightly draped around her shoulders. His other hand cupped her chin and slowly turned her face up to his.

You absolutely cannot kiss him back, Kara warned herself. *He'd take that as confirmation of his screwball ideas, and then you'd really be in the soup.*

Mentally, she braced herself. He might be seductive, demanding, maybe even threatening—but there was no doubt in her mind that he'd do anything in his power to get her to respond. So she must not give him the satisfaction; no matter what sort of self-discipline it took, she would sit like a statue and let him feel as if he were kissing granite. No matter what he did, she'd be cold and inert.

He pushed a lock of hair back from her temple, tucking it behind her ear. Every separate hair seemed to resonate as it slid through his fingers, and it took all of Kara's self-control to stay still.

As he leaned closer, she stopped breathing. Her eyelids

fluttered shut as she tried to deny what was about to happen...

He didn't kiss her. Instead, he leaned very close and whispered, "See you tomorrow." Then the warmth of his touch was gone. She opened her eyes and watched him walk toward the back door. She felt almost dizzy. With relief that he'd gotten the message, she told herself.

The knob clicked as he turned it and Kara suddenly sat up straight. "Wait a minute. You forgot to write those checks after all."

Jax looked over his shoulder; there was a note of admiration in his voice. "You don't miss a thing, do you?" He tossed the checkbook back to her.

"Without your signature, this isn't any good to me."

"But it could be," he murmured. "Mrs. Montgomery... Personally, I think it has a very nice ring to it. A little while ago, you told me to bite the bullet, Kara. Now it's time for you to take a nibble or two, as well. Just look on the bright side, my dear. You may find you like the taste after all."

The Jaguar seemed to steer itself toward a creek where he'd spent a lot of time in his boyhood, fishing rod in hand. Jax sat on the bank, chewing on a stalk of grass, watching the ripples, listening to the music of water against rock.

It had been years since he'd put a line in the water. In fact, he'd almost forgotten just how much he loved to go fishing. He'd never been impatient with the leisurely pace or the long periods of waiting. He'd never been bored by the minute details like choosing precisely the right lure to tempt a particular prey, or by the infinite repetition of slowly dangling the bait, using it to tantalize and entice until experience and instinct told him the moment had come to set the hook and pull the prize into his hands.

This time, of course, his quarry didn't have scales and fins, but long, soft blond hair and enormous green eyes. Still, the principles were the same. He'd give Kara a while to think about the lure, and when the time was right, he'd reel her in. His gut said it wouldn't be long now.

Fishing, he thought, was an awful lot like making love.

He hadn't even touched her mouth—but her lips ached anyway.

Of course, Kara told herself, that was only one of the many paradoxes that flowed in Jax Montgomery's wake. He was a gazillionaire who kept an eye on every penny...but had nevertheless let a beautiful woman inveigle tens of thousands of dollars from him without—apparently—ever asking to see a receipt. He was the grown child of loving parents, who, instead of seeking to emulate their good fortune, was coolly signing on for the modern-day equivalent of a dynastic marriage.

And I'm the chosen bridal sacrifice, Kara thought with a shudder. Even worse, she was merely a casual replacement for his previous, equally chilly choice. She'd happened to show up at the wrong place, at the wrong time...

If I had it to do over again, she reflected grimly, *I'd darn well keep my flashlight in my handbag, instead of jabbing it into his ribs*.

The main attribute Anabel had offered was her beauty, he'd said. He'd been perfectly calm about the assessment; it was apparent that while the woman might have touched his pride—and she'd certainly touched his wallet—Anabel had never touched his heart.

Kara supposed it should be some comfort to know that she was on an equal footing with her predecessor. At least she wasn't following an adored lost love, a woman whose appeal she could never approach.

She realized abruptly that she was acting and thinking as if she'd given in—as if the wedding was still on. As if, now that Anabel was once and for all out of the picture, Kara was stuck.

Which was ridiculous, of course. Jax couldn't force her to marry him. All she had to do was sit down with her list and call the florist, the baker, the caterer, the photographer…

The same people she'd reassured yesterday morning. The same people she'd told that the wedding was going ahead, the bride and groom were perfectly happy together, and everything was fine.

She knew she'd sound like a fool when she called the whole thing off less than forty-eight hours later.

There are worse things, she told herself firmly. Like blithely announcing to everybody that there'd been an abrupt change of bride. Then she'd really look like a blockhead.

On the other hand, unless she stepped into Anabel's shoes, she would have to tell all those people that she still didn't know when or if they were going to be paid—and that was no easy assignment, either.

She put her head down in her hands and groaned.

She couldn't do anything till morning anyway. The business people she dealt with worked every weekend, and they worked hard; Sunday evening was no time to call them at home with problems. Maybe by tomorrow Jax would have reconsidered, relented, realized the risks he was taking with his serendipitous approach to choosing a wife. Maybe by tomorrow she'd figure out an alternative—or at least a more reasonable way of breaking the news.

She'd wait till morning, she decided. Or maybe she'd hold off until she heard from Jax again, to give him every opportunity to regain his senses....

The fact is, you don't want to do anything.

The words rang in her mind like an indictment.

Of course she didn't *want* to do anything, she admitted, because she didn't look forward to sounding foolish, and she was even less fond of appearing unprofessional. But she didn't have any choice; she had to act.

That, however, was part of the problem. Jax had put them in a crunch situation. Something had to be done, but once she'd told the suppliers what was going on, there could be no more changes of mind. They'd all be stuck with the consequences.

So it was only sensible to talk to Jax one last time before she took action, just to be certain that there would be no more surprises down the road.

But it's not that, her conscience whispered. *You don't want to cancel. You want to go straight on.*

You want to marry him.

She was so stunned by the traitorous thought that she said out loud, "That is absolutely ridiculous!"

But true, said the relentless little voice inside her head. *You don't want to solve the problem. You have never wanted to solve the problem. You want to be stuck.*

The ice water trickling down her spine reminded Kara of the first time she'd considered the possibility of marrying him. Even then, she hadn't had any intention of actually doing it; she'd only been thinking of how appalling a notion it was and how glad she felt that she didn't have to take it seriously. But the bare, abstract idea had given her a case of the shivers so cold that Antarctica looked like a tropical resort.

She couldn't possibly be taking his proposal seriously now. Could she?

Remember those shivers, she warned herself, and tried to analyze exactly what she'd been feeling. Had it been fear? Anxiety? Dread?

Or had it been longing? Hope? Anticipation at the idea that someday she might be able to call him her own?

You're losing your mind, she told herself. *You can't have fallen in love with him.*

Once voiced, however—even though it had been in negative terms—the possibility nagged at Kara, turning her thoughts upside down and coloring everything she did. She didn't know how many times she picked up the telephone on Monday morning and then put it down again because she simply couldn't decide what to do.

Cancel the wedding? It was the only sensible action to take. Their so-called engagement had been a fake from the first, a practical joke that had gotten way out of hand long before the discovery of Anabel's embezzlement had turned it suddenly serious. It was absolutely insane for her even to think of going through with it.

Marriages—good marriages—were not built of scams and schemes, coincidences and conspiracies, revenge and retaliation. They were founded on love and respect and trust and friendship—the kinds of things that John and Jeannette Montgomery so clearly displayed. Jax might not understand how special his parents were, but Kara did—and she didn't intend to settle for anything less when it was her turn.

And yet...

There was no denying that she felt more alive in Jax's company than she ever had before. Every nerve ending tingled, every cell stood to attention, not just because she had to watch every word and every step, but because she was also so much more aware not only of him but of her surroundings when he was with her.

When she thought that Anabel would be his bride, Kara had tried to reassure herself that after the wedding she wouldn't have to see him again. But it hadn't been relief she'd felt at the idea; it had been a flat emptiness.

It was true, then. She had fallen in love with him. She looked deep into her soul and admitted that if Jax went out of her life, he would take all the color with him.

But loving him didn't change the circumstances surrounding this oddball engagement. She was his fiancée only by default, because her name and her situation made her, in his opinion, an appropriate sort of wife. It wasn't really *her* he wanted. Anyone in similar circumstances would do; Anabel was proof enough of that.

Which made it more painful yet for Kara to admit that she wanted him. Not the sun king. Not the tycoon. Just Jax. The man who would send half the contents of a gourmet shop to a sweet old lady and purposely arrange it so he wouldn't get credit. The man who bought a string of pearls because, with a careless comment, he'd cost the clerk her commission from another customer. The man who could always make Kara look at the other side of a situation and laugh...

Was it—could it ever be—enough that she cared for him?

Jax had said he'd see her on Monday, but the hours dragged by and there was no sign of him. Kara found herself wondering if it had been only a careless comment, meant more as a general intention than a promise. Or had he said it quite deliberately, with no intention of following through, just to keep her off balance and off guard?

Listen to yourself, Kara thought. If her first reaction—or very nearly her first—was to wonder if he had purposely manipulated her, then where else would her suspicions eventually lead her? Surely if she could doubt him about something so simple, she shouldn't even be contemplating the idea of marrying him.

But telling herself that was one thing. Erasing the love she had so newly discovered was something else.

One thing was sure, she decided. Sitting at home and talking to herself was doing no good; she was only going around in circles. Perhaps when she saw him again, things would become clearer. Now that she understood how she felt, perhaps she would see him in a whole new light—and then she would know what to do.

And as long as she was hoping to observe him with newly cleared vision, why not in a whole new setting, as well? It might be telling, for instance, to see what he was like at work....

Before she could argue herself out of it, Kara looked up the address and found her keys.

When Kara walked into the office complex on the top floor of an old terra-cotta-sheathed building in the center of the city, her first impression was that it could have been there forever. The muted colors, the solid style, even the art on the walls had a sort of timeless flavor. In fact, she thought, there was nothing trendy in the whole suite except the offbeat color of the receptionist's nail polish; in a year, in ten years, in decades, the office would look just as classic.

Her second impression was that the whole place was absolutely crawling with women. Not all of them were young, not all were overwhelmingly feminine or strikingly attractive. But they were everywhere.

The receptionist. The mail clerk who was making deliveries. The power-suited individual beyond the half-open door marked Corporate Counsel. The visitor in a simple olive-green dress, tailored almost like a uniform, who was crossing the waiting room toward the exit as Kara came in. Had Jax deliberately surrounded himself with women?

In the doorway, Kara stopped in her tracks as the visitor called her name. "My dear," Jeannette Montgomery said, "Jax didn't tell me he was expecting you this afternoon. I'm glad I've run into you, though, because his aunts would like to give you a bridal shower—before the wedding if there's time."

"I don't think..." Kara realized too late that she hadn't the foggiest notion where she was headed with that sentence. *I don't think we'll be getting married after all? I don't think there'll be time to fit in another party? I don't think there's anything I can't cancel to accommodate Jax's aunts?* Instead, she said feebly, "*All* his aunts?"

Jeannette smiled and shifted the weight of her shoulder bag. "Every last one—Agnes included. I said I'd ask and get back to them."

"I'll check my calendar." A random thought hit Kara and was off her tongue before she stopped to consider. "Surely you're not thinking of wearing purple for the wedding, are you?"

"I was rather hoping you'd release me from the obligation," Jeannette said dryly. "Anabel seemed to think it was only sporting of me to match."

"Anabel is an idiot. That shade of olive-green you're wearing would be drab on anyone else, but it's great on you. In purple, you'd look—"

"A fright, wouldn't I?"

"Not your best," Kara said tactfully. "I thought, since

your dress wasn't part of the official plan, that you might be bucking the trend.''

"Not a bad idea, at that. Kara, I still think that you should call this whole circus off and have the wedding you want—when you want it. Perhaps I'm being superstitious, but the very idea of simply stepping into another woman's shoes, much less her wedding gown...''

As if I could, Kara almost said. It would take the whole bevy of purple-clad bridesmaids to push her into Anabel's dress, and then if she took a deep breath to say her vows, she wouldn't hear the words but the crack of satin splitting as the dress disintegrated.

The sudden clarity of the image hit Kara like a rock, and she closed her eyes in pain. How could she even have thought of going ahead with the wedding? How could she even have tried to fool herself into believing that a marriage based on such a shaky beginning would have any chance at all of success?

Yes, she loved him—but that didn't make a grain of difference.

"I'm sorry, my dear," Jeannette said gently. "It's between you and Jax, and none of my business. I'll talk to you tonight, if I may?"

Kara nodded, almost absently. *I'll leave him a message*, she thought. *Perhaps it's the coward's way, but...*

The door of the inner office opened, and from the threshold Jax said, "Hello, Kara. This is a nice surprise. Come in."

Maybe it was better this way, she told herself. *Get it out in the open and over with*. Meekly, she followed him into the office.

He closed the door and looked at her.

How was it possible, Kara wondered, that by simply by looking at her, he could make her feel as if her bones were charring, her stomach melting? How could he make her forget the so-sensible decision she'd made, with such good reason, only a couple of minutes before?

Before she realized he was moving, Jax was beside her, his hands cupping her face.

"No," she said breathlessly.

His eyes had darkened. "I don't think you really mean that."

She expected his kiss to be demanding, possessive—as if he was staking a claim. Instead, it was gentle, seeking— as if he was asking a question. Her determination would have strengthened in the face of a demand, but the question drained away her resolve.

She wasn't certain what his question was; she was facing a difficult enough one of her own. Could she simply walk away from this man?

What she couldn't do was stop herself from responding to his kiss; ever since he had left her yesterday without so much as a peck on the cheek, she had been longing for the taste of him. She'd have had to be inhuman to deny herself the satisfaction of this embrace. If she was to have only the memory of him...

His voice was husky. "Make love with me, Kara. Right now."

He might have been reading her mind, Kara thought. If she was to have only the memory of him, why not make it the ultimate remembrance? She loved him, after all...and there was something very flattering about his urgency.

But the last remaining fragment of detachment, of self-preservation, made her challenge him. "Will that satisfy you?"

He didn't even hesitate, but drew her still closer. "Not a chance. But it's a start."

His answer had cleared Kara's mind even though the conclusion she reached was hardly the same one he had. His reasoning was dead on target, she told herself; making love with him—just once—might provide the most satisfying moments of her life, but it would only be a start. It would not assuage the underlying need—only magnify it.

Even with her heightened senses, it took a moment for Kara to recognize a tap on the door and then the click of the latch as it opened. Jax had not been so impaired, however; before the door had swung wide, he'd turned his back, sheltering Kara with the breadth of his shoulders.

"Mr. Montgomery," the secretary said.

Jax's voice was taut. "I do not want to be interrupted."

"I'm not a fool, sir. But under the circumstances I thought you'd fire me for *not* interrupting. Donald Sloan is calling. He said you'd offered him a business proposition and he wants to talk about it."

Kara could feel the tension in the air, in his body. Then his arms dropped away from her. "You're right," he admitted. "I'd have fired you if I'd missed this chance." He looked down at Kara, then said to the secretary, "Stall him for a couple of minutes, will you?"

The secretary muttered something and backed out of the office.

Jax ran a hand through his hair. "I'm sorry, sweetheart—"

"About the interruption itself?" Kara said gently. "Or the fact that your secretary is apparently used to this sort of thing? She didn't even turn a hair."

"Kara—"

"Don't worry, Jax. I wouldn't dream of keeping you from business. Even a couple of minutes could make a difference when it's Donald Sloan on the other end of the line.''

Donald Sloan. *You offered him a business proposition,* the secretary had said.

Donald Sloan, the recluse...the man who seldom agreed to see anybody. So just when—and how—had Jax managed anything of the sort?

When was obvious. On Saturday afternoon, Jax and Donald Sloan, bored with the chat about party arrangements, had wandered off into a corner and talked about Donald Sloan's business.

It was the *how* that bothered Kara—because it was equally obvious.

Jax had volunteered to take her to the Sloans' home. He'd pushed himself into her appointment. He'd seized the opportunity to draw Donald Sloan aside and talk to him...and the topic, she recalled, had been his choice, too. He was the one who'd asked about the razors Donald Sloan manufactured.

"You used me," she said. "You deliberately used me to get to Donald Sloan. To make a business deal. Didn't you?"

Jax took a deep breath, but he didn't have to speak. She could see the answer in his eyes.

CHAPTER NINE

KARA wasn't about to wait around for his admission or the justification that would follow. She didn't need to hear the obvious; Jax had seen an opportunity, and brilliant businessman that he was, he'd gone after it. His action had been as natural—as automatic—as a frog sticking out his tongue to catch a fly.

The fact that along the way he'd trampled Kara's feelings into the mud couldn't be expected to make any difference to him. She could explain it well into next week and he still wouldn't understand. She might as well talk to the frog.

Besides, she realized, if she tried to make him see what he'd done, the only thing she was likely to accomplish was to make Jax wonder why she was reacting so strongly. Why it was so important. Why she was taking his dealings with Donald Sloan as a personal affront.

It wasn't as if Jax had stolen business from her, for they weren't in competition. It wasn't as if he'd cost her work, either; in fact, by suggesting that she handle the fund-raiser for Mrs. Sloan's theater group, he'd gotten her an extra job. Other than that, his interference hadn't affected her professionally at all.

It was purely on a personal level that Kara felt exploited. She had not only learned to care about him, but she had—very imprudently and despite her own common sense—begun to hope that he cared about her. And so, when he treated her like nothing more than a casual busi-

154

ness contact to be capitalized on at the first opportunity…well, was it any wonder she felt insulted?

Of course, if Jax was to realize how very personally she was taking this…

It was bad enough that she'd been so foolish as to dream that the manufactured marriage he'd offered her might ever be a real one. But it would be worse yet if he also realized how very naive she'd been—and worst of all if he was to understand that she'd fallen in love with him.

No matter how callous his action had been, Jax was not at heart an insensitive man. If he stopped to think about it…

It was too late to take back the rash, accusing, full-of-hurt words, so Kara would somehow have to sidetrack any suspicion he might feel. That shouldn't be difficult, she told herself, for he must already be thinking more about Donald Sloan, waiting on the telephone, than about her.

Kara forced herself to smile, though her lips felt as if they would crack from the strain. "How clever of you. What are you going to do anyway—put a solar-powered recharger on his premium razor?" She saw surprise flicker in his eyes, and murmured, "Of course. No wonder you wanted to keep it under wraps. If it's the first thing I thought of, it'll be a natural conclusion for your competitors. Don't keep him waiting, Jax. After all the trouble you took to get him in the mood to talk, I'd hate for you to miss the deal of the century."

She was out of the office before he had a chance to reply—though she suspected he wouldn't have had much to say, and she knew she'd rather not see if there was a glint of relief in his eyes.

Because she wanted so badly to slam the door on her

way out, Kara made it a point to close it very slowly and carefully instead. Only then did she wonder if she looked as disheveled as she felt, but it was too late to do anything about it.

Was it only her imagination that said every woman in the office was eyeing her with expressions ranging from mild curiosity to pure sympathy to the barest hint of incredulity?

I'll never see these people again anyway, she consoled herself. *What they think of me doesn't matter.*

She held her head high as she crossed the office, meeting each gaze firmly and squarely, and didn't let herself sigh with relief until she was out of the building, away from the eyes of all those women....

Away from Jax.

You had a lucky escape, she tried to tell herself.

The evidence of how little she actually meant to him had stung like rubbing alcohol against skin scraped raw. But that pain was nothing compared to how it would have hurt if she'd come slap up against the facts after she'd committed herself to him, or slept with him, or—worst of all—actually married him. She'd let her romantic dreams carry her away like a river in flood; she was fortunate that the raging water had tossed her up on a dry bank before she let herself be swept over the waterfall that waited only a little way downstream. The bump had hurt, to be sure, but better to suffer a few bruises than be caught in a whirlpool with no way out.

For the first time in what seemed a very long while, Kara let herself remember how this had all started—on an ordinary Thursday at the Century Club, when Anabel had caught Jax doing...whatever it was he'd been doing. Kara had almost forgotten about that.

No, she admitted, she hadn't actually forgotten the incident. She'd deliberately put it out of her mind because she hadn't wanted to think about it. She'd wanted to pretend that it hadn't happened, that it didn't matter—that it didn't affect her.

But the discovery that Anabel was so lacking in conscience that she'd stolen from her fiancé was forcing Kara to reassess the episode at the club. She'd known since the day she met Anabel that the woman's top priority was looking out for herself—but Anabel's embezzlement had made it clear precisely how cold-blooded the beauty queen was. An offense that made her lose her temper enough to throw away her chance to be Mrs. Montgomery must have been very bad indeed.

Kara had to admit that she'd still like to know exactly what Jax had done. But in the long run, it didn't matter much. If the chilly Anabel had been incensed by his behavior, then the romantic Kara would have been devastated.

She had told herself that since the incident had happened before she came into the picture, it had nothing to do with her. But what Kara hadn't allowed herself to think about in the past few days was the possibility of that scene—or its equivalent—happening again. She had let her romantic ideas, her attraction to him, her love for him, overcome her common sense. She had let herself believe that her situation was different. She wasn't Anabel—and Jax would change, as well, if it was Kara by his side instead of the beauty queen.

But she'd been fooling herself. Jax was always going to be Jax. And as for the possibility of a recurrence…it would be more accurate to call it a near certainty.

Jax not only hadn't apologized to Anabel for his behavior, but he hadn't even recognized the need to do so.

In fact, he'd acted as if she had no right to object to his extracurricular entertainment.

And since nothing had changed, really—except the identity of the bride—Jax wasn't likely to see things differently now. In his view, Kara would have no more right to an opinion about his activities than he'd granted Anabel.

Her idealistic dreams would have made no impact on Jax at all. She might have been able to keep fooling herself for a while, but the truth was if she had married him, it would have been on his terms. Eventually, Kara would have been forced to face the facts—and admit that she couldn't live with the terms he offered. The longer the self-deception went on, the heavier the eventual price would have been.

Yes, she was fortunate indeed to have escaped long before that, with no more damage than battered pride and a wounded heart.

Now there were only a few loose ends to take care of. Chief among them, of course, was the wedding.

But finally, with the new crystal clarity of her vision, Kara knew exactly what she intended to do about the sun king's wedding.

She'd always been able to find solace in her work, though at first, when Kara settled down at her big worktable to begin her newest task, her mind kept skipping off to Jax and wishing...

No, she told herself firmly. She did *not* wish that the secretary hadn't interfered with their little tête-à-tête. She'd made up her mind even before the interruption that she wasn't going to make love with him no matter how enticing the prospect. The intrusion hadn't changed that, but if his secretary hadn't poked her nose in, Kara would have told Jax about her decision—and probably said a great deal more about her reasons than would have been wise.

So by interrupting, the secretary had actually done her a favor. A couple of them, in fact. Just knowing about Donald Sloan and how Jax had used her to make his business deal was enough to drown the regret Kara might otherwise have felt—someday—about turning him down....

And you, Kara told herself rudely, *can spin a whopper with the best of them.*

She'd have regrets, no matter what. She'd have to be more than human not to wonder what it would have been like to make love with him, not to wish that she'd caught hold of that one precious memory to keep forever close.

But at least she hadn't embarrassed herself by telling him her reasons. At least she'd kept her dignity.

Sooner or later, she'd still have to face him—to tell him about the arrangements she'd made concerning the wedding and to return his diamond ring. But by the time that happened, she'd have had a chance to regain her composure, and with a bit of luck, she'd be able to treat Jax Montgomery like the loose end he was. A casual detail that had to be tended to, not important enough to make a fuss about.

With a bit of luck, she reflected wryly. *And a couple of decades to practice.*

Eventually, Kara settled to her task, becoming so absorbed in the details that she was startled by the doorbell and even more surprised to realize that while she'd been occupied, the afternoon had slid well into evening. The sky was dark, and when she turned on the porch light so she could see who was ringing the bell, the man standing outside put a hand up as if to defend his eyes from the sudden glare.

Her chest suddenly felt constricted, and it was hard to breathe. *Just another loose end*, Kara reminded herself, and opened the door. "I wondered how long it would take you to show up." Her tone was light. "You and Donald must have had a lot to talk about."

Jax's gaze moved slowly over her face. "May I come in?"

"My goodness, it *is* a day of firsts. You, actually asking permission?" She stepped back from the door, leaving him to close it.

Deliberately, she moved back to the big table, sat down, and shifted her papers together. Even a man not known for taking hints could hardly fail to catch the significance of that action, she thought. She might as well have told him, *Say your piece and get out.*

He stood in the center of the room, hands jammed in his pockets. "I'm sorry, Kara."

Her heart skipped a beat. Jax Montgomery, apologizing? *Don't jump to conclusions*, she warned herself. *Just because you can think of about seventeen things he ought to apologize for doesn't mean he's got the whole list in mind*. Determinedly, she kept her voice cool. "For what?"

"Setting you aside today because of business. I shouldn't have done that."

Despite herself, Kara felt disappointment oozing through her veins. Was that all he felt remorseful about? "What happened? Didn't Donald Sloan take up your offer after all?"

"Yes, he did, but I don't see what that has to do with—"

"Don't you? I thought perhaps you were just regretting

that you'd sacrificed the possibility of getting me into bed for a phone call that ended up being nothing important.''

His eyes flashed. ''You're being a bit cynical all of a sudden.''

''Hanging around with you would make anybody a cynic, Jax.''

The silence deepened until it was almost painful. Jax sighed. ''I'm doing this all wrong, aren't I?''

''I've seen better attempts at apologies, yes. If what you're trying to say is that you think I'm angry because you put your business first, you're wrong. You didn't set me aside today—I left. There's a big difference.''

''You took off as if your toes were on fire. What else could I think but that you were angry?''

''That interruption came as something of a relief, actually,'' she said thoughtfully, ''since you obviously weren't in any mood even to discover the reason I was there, much less discuss it.''

He came across the room and perched on the corner of the table at a careful distance from her. ''All right. Here's your chance. What did you come to talk about?''

She lifted her chin and looked straight at him. ''Canceling the wedding.'' There was no apparent reaction; she didn't even see a flicker in his eyes. ''But you suspected that as soon as you saw me, didn't you? That was why you engineered that little... to phrase it loosely...love scene. You were trying to change my mind—again.''

''That wasn't the reason, Kara.''

''Maybe not the only one, but it was right up there in the top three.'' She leaned back in her chair and debated her next move. He deserved to be hit by the biggest possible shock wave—

The telephone chimed, so close to her that it sounded more like a bullhorn. But despite the jolt to her overstimulated nerves, Kara welcomed the interruption; it couldn't have been better timed. She put one hand on the phone and said deliberately, "As a matter of fact, Jax, your little ploy worked. I did change my mind."

He leaned toward her, one hand outstretched.

As if she hadn't seen him move, Kara swiveled her chair away and picked up the phone. It was, as she half expected, Jeannette Montgomery, asking about the bridal shower.

Jax slid off the table and came to stand behind her, resting his hands gently on Kara's shoulders. She did her best to ignore him though the warmth of his touch seemed to burn through the thin silk of her blouse.

"Please tell the aunts there's no need for a shower, Jeannette," Kara said. "I've been thinking about your advice—what you said about stepping into another woman's shoes, I mean—and I decided that you're right. It would be very distasteful indeed, and so I'm not going to do it."

Jeannette was silent for a moment. "I think that's a very wise choice," she said finally. "If you need help with anything at all—notifying guests, dealing with details…"

"I'll call you," Kara promised. She put the phone down.

Jax's hands were still resting on her shoulders, but he was no longer massaging her muscles; it felt instead as if she were balancing a couple of bricks. Kara didn't move.

"You told my mother you were calling it off," he said slowly. "But you just told me—"

"No." Kara shook her head. "What I told her was that I didn't intend to be a substitute bride at Anabel's wedding."

Slowly, his fingers began to move again, stroking the

tight muscles in her shoulders. "I thought for a minute you were backing out altogether." His voice was as warm and caressing as his hands. "But as long as it's just a matter of changing some of the arrangements so it doesn't feel like the wedding Anabel planned—"

"How gracious of you to allow me a say," Kara murmured. "But as a matter of fact, that's not what I meant at all. Anabel's wedding is going to take place almost exactly the way Anabel planned it. Except neither Anabel nor I will be wearing that dress."

"So what are you planning to do now?" A note of amusement had crept into his voice. "You can't just grab somebody off the street and set her in front of the altar with me."

"Why not?" Kara asked dryly. "*You* did—more or less. But you're quite right, come to think of it, because the average woman on the street would have even more trouble getting into that dress than I would."

His fingertips brushed down the length of her arm, and his hand cupped hers, lifting the diamond ring she wore into the glow of the desk lamp. "You're still my fiancée, Kara."

"Now that's where you're wrong. The only reason the ring is still on my finger is because it's safer there." She slid the diamond off her hand and turned to face him, holding it out. "I considered leaving it with your secretary this afternoon just to get rid of it a little earlier, but I didn't want you to blame her for this mess any more than you already did."

He looked down at the diamond and then at Kara. "But you said you're not going to cancel. So—"

"There will be a wedding," she said. "At least, it will look like a wedding—and it will be followed by a reception, complete with the six kinds of cake Anabel ordered.

But instead of sending gifts, the guests will be buying tickets. The price of admission will go to Mrs. Sloan's theater group, and the actors will play all the parts. Unless, of course, you'd like to pretend to be the groom—because that will be as close as you'll get to being married that day.''

Jax's mouth had set into a grim line.

"You did want me to arrange Mrs. Sloan's fundraiser,'' Kara reminded him. "You suggested it purely in order to impress Donald, I realize now, and as it turns out, you were very successful. She's delighted with the idea, and I'm sure she'll tell her husband and you'll get all the credit.''

Jax pressed two fingers to his forehead, right above the bridge of his nose, and shook his head as if it hurt.

"Besides,'' Kara went on, "as you told me just the other day, it's for a good cause. So if you'd really like to be noble—and impress the Sloans even more while you're at it—you can pay off the bills that are still outstanding and consider the money a contribution to the theater group.''

Jax muttered, "And write the whole thing off on my income tax as a charitable donation.''

"You never miss a trick, do you?'' She took a malicious delight in quoting his own words back at him. "I ought to have expected that, of course. When it comes to money, there's nobody faster on the draw than you are, Jax. Or you can remain the stiff-necked, stubborn fool you are, ignore your moral obligation to take care of the bills you owe, and we'll pay the rest of the costs out of the ticket sales. I don't really care. Mrs. Sloan might, I imagine—but what you do isn't any of my affair anymore.''

"And you're pleased.''

"Was there ever any doubt?" She looked him straight in the eye and was startled by the suspicion she saw lurking there. If, despite all her efforts, he was wondering about her motives, she had to put a stop to that sort of speculation, and the sooner the better. Where the words came from, she wasn't certain, but they tripped off her tongue as if they'd been rehearsed. "But that's not really fair of me—to say I never wanted anything but to get out of this mess. Because I *was* tempted for a bit, Jax. It would've been such a sensible move to marry you."

"What changed your mind?" His tone was almost casual.

"I think it was my grandparents' example. That was such a sensible marriage, too—and look how it ended up."

"A couple of snobs who thought they were too good for the world."

"Oh, that was only the public side of them." Kara's voice dripped irony. "If you think the tension was thick when they went to the Century Club, you should've seen them at home. They thought they were too good for each other, too. Each of them thought they had settled for far too little—and they nagged at each other all the time."

Jax's eyebrows lifted slightly. "No wonder your father was so spineless he couldn't make a decision. And no wonder you took all those golf lessons when you came to visit them."

"You're right. It was a way to stay out of the house. And that's why I'm not interested—no matter how sensible an idea it might have seemed."

The silence drew out painfully. *Why doesn't he just leave?* Kara wondered. She fiddled with the papers on her desk to avoid looking at him again, and the corner of a brown leather folder peeked out at her. "Oh—your checkbook," she said, reaching for it. "You'll find it in exactly the same condition you left it. Now if you don't mind—"

He took the folder and twisted it in his hands. "Kara, if we could just—"

"There is no *we*, Jax. Now if you'll excuse me—I need to start calling all the guests on your invitation list."

"It isn't necessary for you to do that, surely."

"Are you volunteering to help? Or merely suggesting that we not bother to notify them at all? Actually, though, I'm not calling to tell them your wedding's off. It's a built-in database of possible contributors. Since they're already planning to come to a wedding, I'll just ask if, instead of a gift, they'd mind buying a ticket."

"I'm surprised you didn't ask my mother if she'd like to attend."

"Oh, I'll ask. I thought it only fair to let you be the first to know about the arrangements, since it was your wedding."

"You mean, you told me first—after Mrs. Sloan?"

"Well, of course," Kara said lightly. "I had to be sure she was interested. There's just one last thing before you go, Jax—the pearls you bought as a bride's gift." She almost choked on the words. *I could have been the bride. His bride...* "I don't suppose you'd consider donating them to the cause as a raffle prize?"

"Would you buy a chance if I did?"

She looked at him, wide-eyed. "Why on earth would I want them?" *They'd only be a painful reminder—and I have enough of those already.*

"I can't think of a single reason," he said. "Maybe I'll see you at the wedding."

The wedding that could have been ours... Stop it! she told herself frantically. *You're only prolonging the pain.*

"It'll be fun to see what they do with it," she said

quietly. "And you don't have to decide ahead of time, Jax. You can buy a ticket at the door."

He sat on the stream bank, turning the diamond ring back and forth in his hand and looking from its fiery heart to where sunshine sparkled on the rippling waters.

As soon as Kara had walked out of his office, Jax had known it hadn't been wise to let her go. He just hadn't realized how massive a mistake it had been.

Of course, even if he could have prevented her from leaving, there hadn't been much he could say. He hadn't had a lot of alternatives when it came to explaining himself. He could hardly say he didn't know what the secretary was talking about, or that he didn't have any business deal pending with Donald Sloan. Kara would have spit in his face if he'd tried any such nonsense, and she'd have been well justified.

And the only real option open to him—making a clean breast of it—would probably have been equally as useless. He'd pretty much have been telling her what she'd already figured out for herself anyway. She wouldn't have given him much credit for the virtue of honesty if he'd confessed only after he'd been caught.

But who would have thought she'd take it all so seriously?

So, like a patient fisherman, he'd given her the freedom to run. It was perfectly safe to do so, he'd told himself, since the hook was still set. He'd give her time to cool off, to think it over, maybe to run herself into exhaustion. Perhaps then she'd listen to reason. He'd wait her out and then he'd cautiously, one slow step at a time, draw her back to him.

Only the hook hadn't been set as firmly as he'd

hoped—and she'd not only wriggled away, she'd splashed his error in his face.

He wasn't turning out to be much of a fisherman after all, Jax thought. In fact, at the moment, he felt a whole lot more like the fish—neatly filleted and sizzling in the frying pan.

It wasn't a lot of comfort to know that he was the one who'd put himself there.

Kara didn't run to the window to watch him go, but it took self-restraint to stay in her chair.

Fool, she told herself. *You were still hoping, weren't you?*

Despite all her logic, she had still been nourishing a fragment of wishful thinking deep in her heart. Perhaps there was an explanation. If he cared enough to try to patch things up...

Now, with the last remnant of foolish hope crushed, she knew there was no sense in delaying. She'd made her list of the things she needed to do to transform Anabel's wedding into Mrs. Sloan's fund-raiser; now it was time to act. Time to set the last bridge between her and Jax afire. Perhaps when she smelled the smoke—hot and thick and choking—her decision would finally feel as real and inevitable as in fact it was.

She didn't regret what she'd done—not any of it. What she regretted was the might-have-been—what they could have shared if only he'd cared about her, too.

But there was no sense in thinking about that, when there were things that needed doing. She picked up the phone and rang the first guest on the list.

And as she waited for the call to go through, she found herself hoping that Jax would have the decency to stay away from the wedding. It was hard enough to say good-bye to him in her heart. If she had to do it in public—at the altar where they might have sealed their lives together—it would rip her apart.

CHAPTER TEN

JUST because it wasn't to be a real wedding after all didn't mean that there were fewer details to be taken care of or fewer tasks to accomplish as the hour drew near. Most of the time, Kara welcomed the mind-numbing pace. At any given moment, there were ten things…ranging from normal checkups to looming catastrophes…waiting for her attention, which meant she didn't have any time left over to think. And that was all to the good.

This time tomorrow, it will be over, she reminded herself as she helped Rhonda load the last plastic-draped bridesmaid's dress into her car. She shoved at the billowing gown till the door closed and watched as Rhonda strapped the baby into his seat. "Are you certain you can handle unloading all these at the Century Club?"

"If I can't, I'll hunt down some busboys and borrow their muscles. Don't worry about it, Kara."

"I could take the baby for a while if it would help you out."

"What you need to take," Rhonda said firmly, "is not Dylan, but a nap."

"I don't have time. I still have to talk to the photographer again because he doesn't seem to understand the change in plans, check how the dance band's doing with the new music and…"

"Well, maybe you should leave the photographer and the dance band to do their jobs and make time for a rest. You've looked like a zombie for the past week or more." Rhonda fiddled with her keys and said, too casually,

"Ever since the sun king stopped hanging around, as a matter of fact."

Kara's stomach tightened. "I told you all about that. It never was anything serious."

"That ring looked pretty serious to me."

"It was nothing but a stage prop. And once it was finally clear to Jax that no matter what happened, he and Anabel were not ever going to patch things up…"

"I'm still not quite straight on exactly how that happened, you know."

"It doesn't matter. You'll get the rest of your money, and that's all that's really important." Kara turned back toward her half of the duplex. "See you tomorrow morning at the Century Club. I'll be there at the crack of dawn, but you won't have to show up till the bridesmaids do…in case they need last-minute adjustments."

"What do you mean, *in case*? And I already have. Gotten the money, I mean."

Kara frowned. "When did that happen?"

"Jax's secretary called a few days ago, asked what the remaining balance was and sent a check. It was hand delivered yesterday. I figured you knew about it."

Kara shook her head.

"Though now that I think it over," Rhonda mused, "she was asking about the other suppliers, too. I just assumed she didn't want to bother you again to verify your list."

"I haven't given anybody a list…either of suppliers or outstanding balances."

Rhonda put both hands to her face in mock horror. "You mean I could've given her any number at all and she didn't have a way of finding out if I was telling the truth? There went my best chance of funding Dylan's college education…down the drain." She grinned. "I'd better get going before he starts chewing on the dresses. Get some sleep, Kara, or at least eat something. If you lose any more weight, you *will* fit into Anabel's gown.''

''Except it would still be about six inches too long.'' Kara waved and headed for her own car. Anabel's dress was also an item on her list for today, and it was probably the most pleasant of them all. Since Mrs. Gleason didn't drive, Kara had said she'd pick up the gown and deliver it to the Century Club, and Mrs. Gleason would no doubt make her a cup of tea and insist that she sit still for a few minutes to drink it.

''Tomorrow it will all be over,'' she muttered, and tried to pretend it was true. The wedding itself would be a thing of the past, of course, with all its excitement and confusion and last-minute panic, leaving only the mopping-up to finish next week. But as for the rest of the fallout from this affair...

She wondered how long it would take to forget about Jax. A century or two?

Mrs. Gleason's door was locked. Kara felt like growling. She realized missing the woman was largely her own fault; she could hardly expect Mrs. Gleason to stay home all day waiting when Kara hadn't given her a specific time. But even if Kara had made a firm appointment, she'd probably have been unable to keep it; in the last hours before a production of this size, there was no predicting how long anything would take.

She was debating whether to stop by again later or just to wait in the lobby...on the theory that wherever Mrs. Gleason had gone, she'd be back soon...when the lock clicked and the door opened.

Mrs. Gleason, Kara saw with concern, looked even shakier than usual; her hands were trembling and her voice held an odd tremor. "My dear," she said, "I'm so glad you've come."

Kara stepped over the threshold into a stream of sunlight that poured through the wide windows, so bright it was almost blinding. "And I'm glad you've started being more careful about locking your..." She stopped dead as a man moved out of the pool of light.

"Hello, Kara," Jax said softly.

You knew this had to happen sometime, she reminded herself. *At least it's here, with only one very innocent old lady to see, and not in front of a crowd at the wedding tomorrow.* "I'm sorry to interrupt your conversation," she said, and waved a casual hand at the bundle that hung on a hook near the door, covered with an all-concealing white linen bag. "I just stopped to pick up the dress."

"Nonsense," Mrs. Gleason said briskly. "You're just in time for an early tea...and you look as if you could use a little fattening up."

"No, please, don't put yourself to any trouble."

"It's no trouble." Mrs. Gleason pointed at the tray balanced on the low table in front of the sofa. "I'll make some fresh tea. Sit down and help yourself to the goodies in the meantime." She disappeared into the kitchen before Kara could protest again.

She sighed. "I should just...I'm running way behind schedule, and..."

"She'd be very disappointed if you left," Jax said.

He sounded perfectly calm about it...but of course he would, Kara thought irritably. He didn't have any personal stake in whether she stayed. His only concern was Mrs. Gleason's feelings.

"Are you all right?" Jax asked. "You look tired."

Kara sat down and reached for a delicate chocolate

straw. "I'm perfectly fine," she said crisply. "But I'm sorry to see you're off your food."

Jax frowned. "What makes you think…"

"There are three whole cream puffs left on the tray." Kara pointed. "Do you have a headache or something?" Attacking him, she reminded herself, was no way to maintain the air of aloofness that was so important right now. She sighed. "Sorry. I shouldn't take it out on you. I suppose I'm having a reaction to spending half an hour on the phone this morning explaining to your mother why I didn't think it was a good idea for me to come to dinner tonight."

"She's not taking this very well," Jax agreed.

"That's sort of like saying Death Valley's a bit warm. Why she so much as considered inviting me to what was supposed to be the rehearsal dinner…Why is she even still having it?"

"Because a lot of the Montgomerys who were invited to the wedding decided to come for the weekend anyway."

"There are *more* of you?"

Jax shrugged. "Here and there. And since she'd already hired the caterer, and everybody needs to eat…"

"I can understand all that. I just couldn't make her see that it would be in very poor taste for me to show up."

"She likes you."

"I like her too, but I don't think…" *And just why couldn't you be friends with her now if the engagement didn't mean anything to you?* The question echoed in her head. Kara only hoped it wouldn't occur to Jax, and she did her best not to leave him time to think about it. "Mrs. Sloan told me you and Donald had cut the deal."

"Yeah."

He didn't sound as pleased as Kara would have expected, but perhaps he thought she was still annoyed over his deception and likely to make yet another fuss about it. She kept her voice determinedly cheerful. "Well, I'm glad something positive came out of all this."

"There's also the windfall for the theater group, of course. How are things going?"

"Pretty well, I think…though perhaps I should warn you that they intend to carry it off as sort of an improvised burlesque of a wedding. One of the bridesmaids had Rhonda sew white elastic panels into the sides of the darkest purple dress so she could stuff it with pillows and appear to be nine months pregnant. I have no idea if she's intending to give birth during the reception, but I wouldn't put it past her."

Jax grinned. "This I have to see."

"I shouldn't expect that you'd want to." *Why do you think I told you, anyway? So you'd stay away, dammit.*

She shifted restlessly. Where was Mrs. Gleason, for heaven's sake? The woman couldn't still be waiting for water to boil…unless she'd forgotten to turn on the stove.

"I don't see why I shouldn't enjoy the show," Jax said. "I don't have any personal feelings about it."

Kara didn't doubt he was telling the truth, and yet it annoyed her that all of a sudden he had so easily let go of something he'd clung to before. "You could have fooled me, the way you insisted on sticking with every detail."

"I didn't, you know. All you had to do was ask. Any change you wanted would have been fine with me."

Kara's breath caught in her throat. *Any change you wanted…* Except the one that mattered most. What difference did dresses and flowers and music make when caring was absent?

"Obviously," he went on, "I didn't make myself clear about that."

"No, you didn't."

His voice was husky. "Would it have made a difference, Kara? If I'd told you to change anything you liked?"

"Except for a few small items, of course...like the date and the place and the general style of things." Kara shook her head. "No, it wouldn't have made a difference."

It would only have made things harder on me if it had been my own wedding...my simple, elegant, peaceful wedding...that I was giving up, instead of Anabel's rodeo show.

"Of course not," Jax said. "I suppose that's why I never thought to be specific about it. Whenever we got close to the subject, you told me once again that you couldn't wait to escape the nightmare."

"Well, I couldn't," Kara said coolly. "It was nice of you to come to pay the rest of Mrs. Gleason's bill yourself."

Jax's eyebrows rose. "How do you know that's why I'm here?"

"The people I work with do talk to me occasionally, so I heard about your paying up." Half-consciously, she picked up another chocolate straw and twisted the delicate pastry into crumbs. "You know, Jax, you could've saved us both a whole lot of aggravation if you'd just done that up front. It was all I asked for, that day on the driving range. In fact, I didn't ask for that much, just the cancellation fees."

"Oh, but you hadn't figured out how to make it all deductible yet. Once you did that..."

That figured, she thought. "I have absolutely no doubt you'll be flippant at your own funeral, Montgomery. Tell me one thing, will you? When did you decide to use me to get to Donald Sloan? Right after I stuck the flashlight in your ribs, when I first mentioned him?''

He sighed. ''Along about then. Though I think it's putting it a bit strongly to say I used you.''

''Oh, I don't think so. Is that why you suggested the pretense of an engagement in the first place...to give yourself a better chance to make contact with him? How far would you have carried it, Jax? As far as you had to, I suppose. Even to the altar if he hadn't come through before then.''

''It's two different things, Kara.''

''Both of them manipulative and hurtful...and wrong.''

He held up a hand in a sort of warning. ''Not telling you why I wanted to get to Donald Sloan...you're correct about that. It was wrong. But that had nothing to do with the engagement. And it didn't make the wedding a bad idea.''

''Or a good one, either.'' Kara jumped up. ''I really can't wait any longer. Tell Mrs. Gleason I'm sorry, will you? I'll just snag Anabel's...I mean, the dress off the hook and...''

''Don't, Kara.'' He stood up, too, hands out as if to hold her back.

She shot a quizzical look at him. ''Why not? It's ready to go.'' She lifted the white linen bag down from the hook, a bit surprised by how light it was; she'd expected a far bulkier, heavier package. Before that fact really registered, however, the concealing linen slid down from the top of the hanger, threatening to drop away entirely.

''Or maybe it wasn't ready to go,'' Kara said wryly. ''I should've checked to make sure the bag was tied up tight.'' She put the hanger back on the hook and caught with both hands at the bag to draw it back up over the bodice of the dress.

Only then did she realize that it wasn't Anabel's dress. Not only had it not been bulky or heavy enough, it was a completely different style and not even the same color; instead of white, this dress was the shade of rich, thick cream.

Getting to the Century Club with the wrong wedding gown would have been a big enough problem, she thought, even though the theater group was showing itself able to innovate even when faced with the weirdest of circumstances.

But if the bride who intended to wear this dress found it missing, she'd be facing a disaster. To a woman who had commissioned a Roaring Twenties–style dress...cut of ivory silk, complete with fringe and beads...being left with Anabel's gown would not be the least bit amusing.

A Roaring Twenties dress. Ivory silk. Fringe and beads... The very thing Mrs. Gleason had wanted to make for Kara herself.

Slowly, she pulled the linen bag down until the entire dress was revealed down to the hemline, where six inches of silky fringe pretended to bring the short skirt to a decent length.

"I didn't know Mrs. Gleason was working on another wedding right now," Kara said quietly.

There was a long silence before Jax said, "You weren't supposed to know."

She closed her eyes against the hot prickle of tears. *My wedding dress*, she thought. *He had her make my wedding dress...*

"The door was locked because she was expecting you, and I didn't want you to walk in and see...that."

Kara swallowed hard. "If it was such a secret, why did you ask her to make it?"

"I didn't intend it to be a secret. If you'd shown any inclination along the way to do anything but fight the idea of marrying me, I'd have brought you here and showed it to you."

"But in the meantime, you kept on pushing the original arrangements, the original schedule..."

"As far as the timing, it seemed to be the sensible thing to do. People all over the country had already made travel plans and... It sounds pretty stupid, doesn't it?"

"No. It sounds just like you...efficient and aware of the last dime."

"I always intended to pay the bills, Kara...as soon as I realized you really didn't have the money."

"But you kept hanging them over my head. Why? Was it just for kicks?"

"It seemed to be the only way to get you to take me seriously. If it hadn't been for the possibility of your friends not getting their money, you'd have tossed me out on my ear long ago."

He'd wanted her to take him seriously. He'd wanted to marry her....

It doesn't change anything, Kara thought. He hadn't said any more, really, than on the Sunday night when she'd discovered Anabel's embezzlement and he'd told her how sensible it would be for him to marry Kara instead. This was just part of the same package, based on logic instead of love...and faulty logic at that. The fact that he'd shown more sensitivity than she'd expected about the arrangements didn't make any difference whatsoever.

Her hands were trembling too much to fit the linen bag back on the dress, so she folded it up instead and laid it on a nearby table. Her fingertips brushed over the fine, silky fringe, and she gritted her teeth and tried not to see the picture that insisted on forming in her mind...of her wearing that dress, standing beside Jax and promising her life and her love to him....

Nothing had changed, she reminded herself. Nothing at all.

As she started across the room, Jax asked, "Where are you going?"

"To find Mrs. Gleason and ask where Anabel's dress is. And then I'm leaving."

"Please don't, Kara."

Puzzled, she turned slowly to face him. There had been a note in his voice that she'd never heard before.

"I've done this all wrong, haven't I?" he said. "I should have told you."

"Told me what? About Donald Sloan? I was furious for a while about that, I admit it."

Jax shook his head. "How I felt. Not that it would've made any difference, I suppose, but at least I'd have given it my best shot instead of waiting...and hoping...that you'd see the advantages..."

"If you say another word about advantages," Kara threatened, "I'll choke you with a cream puff." She pushed open the swinging door to the kitchen. "Mrs. Gleason?"

"She's not there. She went out the back door so I'd have a chance to talk to you."

"Your idea, or hers?"

"A little of both. There are some things I need to tell you, Kara. Things I should've said a long time ago. Do you want to know why I kept talking about all the advantages of marrying me? Because I thought if I told you I'd fallen in love with you, even your friends' money wouldn't have kept you from disappearing in a cloud of dust.''

Kara's hand slipped, and the door would have smacked her in the face if Jax hadn't caught it and eased her out of its path.

"What do you mean…love?" she said breathlessly. "You can't expect me to believe that you…when you arranged a pretend engagement so you could get Anabel back…"

"Nope. You assumed that's what I was doing. And I figured anything that kept you close to me…let you get used to the idea of me…was worth trying."

"You…"

"Think about it, Kara. What would you have done if I'd told you that, well, yes, up till a half hour before I met you, I *was* engaged to another woman, but really…honest and truly…I fell in love with you at first sight?"

She could hardly breathe. "I'd say you were a liar…and not a very smooth one."

"Exactly. And as a matter of fact, that wasn't quite what happened."

Her heart twisted painfully. *What a fool you are to get your hopes up once more, only to have them smashed again.*

"I don't think I truly fell in love till the moment I realized that you'd stuck me up with a flashlight."

She shook her head a little, trying to clear the buzz from her ears. "You have a flashlight fetish or something?"

"It was gutsy, and creative, and utterly charming…both the stickup and your reasons for doing it. And falling in love like that is a characteristic of the

Montgomery men. It hits…as you put it…like lightning. Suddenly, and forever.''

She frowned. ''Then how do you explain Anabel?''

''Oh, yes. Anabel.'' He sighed. ''You asked once if I didn't want what my parents have. Yes, I do. But I'm thirty-two, Kara. I thought I'd missed the gene for the love-at-first-glimpse phenomenon. And so, if I wasn't going to find a woman I could love like that, I decided to be sensible about my choice. Anabel was suitable, appropriate and decorative.''

''What else could you ask for in a bride?'' Kara said wryly.

''You.''

She felt as if the breath had been knocked out of her. Was all of this possible?

''Everything I found out about you…watching you with my parents, with Rhonda's baby, even at that deafeningly awful nightclub…only made me more certain of my feelings. Kara,'' he said softly, ''I won't pressure you…I promise. But I'm not giving you up, either. Let me have a chance to prove how much I care, sweetheart.''

''What have you got in mind?''

''Seeing each other. Doing things together. Being friends. For a start, will you think about coming to the dinner tonight? Not as my fiancée…just as a friend. I've learned my lesson about rushing things, Kara. If it takes a year…five years…I don't care. I've gone about it all wrong. I was so afraid if I didn't capitalize on the chance I'd been given that I'd lose you.''

''That's why you pushed so hard to keep the wedding date?''

He nodded. ''I was blinded, I think, by the strength of my own feelings, and afraid you'd turn me down flat before I had a chance to show you what we could have together. That's why I kept talking about the advantages, I suppose. I was hoping to sweep you into marrying me before you had a chance to think it through. And I was trusting that afterward you'd come to care about me the way I already knew I cared about you.''

"Half an hour after breaking up with Anabel." Kara shook her head skeptically.

"You don't believe a word I've said, do you?"

"That's the price you pay for storytelling," Kara pointed out. "You have to admit, Jax, when you get wound up you make Machiavelli look like a straight-line thinker."

"If I was spinning a story, I'd be sure it was logical."

"Well, there's no doubt this one doesn't make sense. I want to trust you, Jax, really I do. But how can you be sure you didn't just fall for me...or think you did...on the rebound? And...well, dammit, what *did* you do that made Anabel so angry?"

"Just between you and me?"

Kara stared at him in disbelief. "And who else would I want to have possession of the details?"

"I told Anabel the engagement was off."

"Is *that* all? Well, at least I have the comfort of knowing it won't happen again...you did *what*?"

"I told her I didn't want to marry her. There was a little matter of a last fling she'd had with an old boyfriend..."

"And you objected? What a piker."

Jax shook his head. "It didn't bother me at all, which made me conclude it was a good idea to get out of the engagement."

"Sounds reasonable to me," Kara muttered.

"I thought, since it was my idea to break it off, that it would be only fair if I took the blame. It wouldn't be very gentlemanly of me to make an issue of her boyfriend, after all."

"She didn't think that…along with keeping her ring…constituted an adequate apology?"

"Not exactly. I knew she wasn't going to like it, of course. That's why I took her off to a private room at the Century Club instead of telling her at her apartment. I thought she might make a little less of a scene at the club than she would if absolutely no one was around, but I was obviously wrong about that, too."

"No wonder she was spitting nails." Now it all made sense. In fact, Kara realized, it was the only way to explain the essential idiocy of Anabel's losing her temper like that. No matter what kind of orgy she'd discovered him in, Anabel would have smiled coolly and tolerated it rather than risk her position. Jax's breaking off the engagement was the one thing she couldn't possibly have put up with.

Or changed either. She'd tried almighty hard, though, draping herself over him after the supposed kidnapping incident and pleading about how she'd learned her lesson. She must have been hoping Jax had been jolted badly enough by the incident to look at things differently, too.

But by then, he'd met Kara…and in that flash of lightning…

She could understand the suddenness of it now that she'd had a chance to think it over. For even though she hadn't recognized what was happening to her, at the time she, too, had suffered that instantaneous attraction. She'd gone out to the driving range to try to talk him into a reconciliation with Anabel, but by the time they were driving to Mrs. Gleason's half an hour later, she'd already concluded that the wedding was off, no matter what. Deep inside, she'd been anxious for it to be canceled, because...even then...she'd been subconsciously wanting him for herself.

She looked into his eyes, and whatever he saw in her face softened the stress lines in his. "Give me a chance, Kara?"

"I think," she said slowly, "that I could be persuaded."

Kissing him was even better, she decided, now that all the games were over and done with. But it was more terrifying, too, in an erotic sort of way, to know that his control was hanging on as thin a thread as her own.

"I have some time off scheduled next week that I was intending to use for a honeymoon," Jax murmured. "If you'd like to go with me..."

She pulled back a little and planted both hands on his chest. "I thought you weren't going to be pushy."

"I said I wouldn't push you about a wedding," he argued. "I figure we can have the honeymoon first and then discuss..."

"I know. Since you've already paid for the tickets, you don't want to waste them."

"I'm not really a miser, you know," Jax complained. "Though, to tell the truth, I'm not exactly a gazillionaire, either."

"Rhonda will be disappointed. She was absolutely certain."

"There are gazillions floating around, I admit, and I pay myself a very nice salary..."

"You must, if you didn't feel any real pain from all the cash Anabel was soaking up."

"But most of the profits from my business go into a charitable trust. That's why my mother was in the office that day...looking over the grant requests for this fiscal year."

You forgot your list, he'd told Jeannette. "She manages it?"

"She was the logical choice since it was her idea."

He'd said something before, she thought vaguely, about Jeannette telling him he had much better uses for his money than buying his parents a new house....

Kara stood on tiptoe to kiss him, and as she settled back into the comfort of his arms, the ivory silk dress hanging near the door caught her eye. "Jax, what are you going to do with that dress?"

"Take it home. You suggested once that I keep a wedding gown in my closet in case I needed it in a hurry someday."

"Good thinking," Kara murmured, "if I do say so myself. What's your definition of a hurry?"

"The instant you say the word. So...since I intend to be doing everything in my power to convince you to marry me sooner or later, I plan to be prepared to act on a moment's notice. Dress, pearls...anything else I should have on hand?"

Her heart was beating so fast she was amazed she could still speak. "I shouldn't think so. It's really not a very *formal* gown, is it?"

"Not exactly, I suppose. Mrs. Gleason wanted to make it long, but the idea of hiding your legs..."

"So it wouldn't have to be a terribly grand occasion, either...right?"

"As long as the people we care about are there...and as long as I have time to get the florist to put your flashlight in the middle of a bouquet..."

"You told me you didn't have it!"

"I said I didn't *take* it. When you mentioned it was missing, I checked the Jaguar and found it under the front seat."

"And kept it in self-defense, I suppose?" Kara rubbed her nose against his shirt collar. "I do love you, you know."

She saw the glitter of gratification in his eyes, and then he was kissing her once more, so long and so intensely that she thought every cell in her body would burst with happiness. When she could breathe again, Kara asked unsteadily, "Is your great-uncle the judge coming to dinner tonight?"

He stared down at her. "Are you saying…"

"I told you there wasn't a chance of your getting married tomorrow," she pointed out. "I didn't say anything about tonight. And it would be a shame to waste the honeymoon tickets."

"A woman after my own heart," Jax said, and rubbed his chin thoughtfully against her hair. "You once said that only an idiot doesn't feel afraid of marriage, Kara, because of the enormous changes and commitments it involves. Well, then—I'm an idiot, because I'm not afraid. Not with you."

"Me, neither," she whispered, and drew him down to her for a kiss to seal the bargain.

What happens when you suddenly discover your happy twosome is about to turn into a...*family*?
Do you laugh?
Do you cry?
Or...do you get married?

The answer is all of the above—and plenty more!

Share the laughter and tears with
Harlequin Romance® as these
unsuspecting couples have to be

READY FOR BABY

When parenthood takes you by surprise!

Authors to look out for include:

Caroline Anderson—DELIVERED: ONE FAMILY
Barbara McMahon—TEMPORARY FATHER
Grace Green—TWINS INCLUDED!
Liz Fielding—THE BACHELOR'S BABY

Available wherever Harlequin books are sold.

HARLEQUIN®
Makes any time special ™

NEARLYWEDS

Almost at the altar— will these *nearly*weds become *newly*weds?

Harlequin Romance® is delighted to invite you to some special weddings! Yet these are no ordinary weddings. Our beautiful brides and gorgeous grooms only *nearly* make it to the altar—before fate intervenes.

But the story doesn't end there....
Find out what happens in these tantalizingly emotional novels!

Authors to look out for include:

Leigh Michaels—The Bridal Swap
Liz Fielding—His Runaway Bride
Janelle Denison—The Wedding Secret
Renee Roszel—Finally a Groom
Caroline Anderson—The Impetuous Bride

Available wherever Harlequin books are sold.

HARLEQUIN®
Makes any time special ™

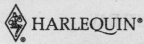

HARLEQUIN®

makes any time special—online...

eHARLEQUIN.com

your romantic life

Romance 101
♥ Guides to romance, dating and flirting.

Dr. Romance
♥ Get romance advice and tips from our expert, Dr. Romance.

Recipes for Romance
♥ How to plan romantic meals for you and your sweetie.

Daily Love Dose
♥ Tips on how to keep the romance alive every day.

Tales from the Heart
♥ Discuss romantic dilemmas with other members in our Tales from the Heart message board.